Dizzy's

JOIE DE VIVRE

JACQUELINE LINDENFELD

ISBN 978-1-64670-581-8 (Paperback)
ISBN 978-1-64670-582-5 (Hardcover)
ISBN 978-1-64670-583-2 (Digital)

Covenant Books, Inc.
11661 Hwy 707
Murrells Inlet, SC 29576
www.covenantbooks.com

ACKNOWLEDGMENTS

The main character ("Dizzy") in this novel is partially based on my own life experience in the United States and France. The other characters, including the cat, are pure products of my imagination. So are many invented situations and details in this book.

Many thanks to my wonderful personal editor Teresa Welch (Wild Iris Communications), who did a great job correcting my French-influenced English and improving many details in my manuscript. I also want to thank my daughter Anne Lindenfeld and her husband Ryland Thompson for their constructive criticism of my manuscript and their technical help.

I am grateful for stimulation and advice from various fellow writers and guest lecturers, especially in the Willamette Writers on the River association in Corvallis, Oregon.

Finally, I owe many thanks to Covenant Books, Inc., for their diligent work to bring this book to publication.

CHAPTER 1

"Devil! Devil! Devil!"

Sam turned his head to see who was shouting on the street in midafternoon. He assumed it was some teenager who was relieved that school was over for the day. To his surprise, he saw a petite, elderly lady walking briskly on the opposite sidewalk. She was dressed casually but neatly: tight jeans, dark blue winter jacket, orange gloves, and a black-and-white Peruvian hat partly covering her curly white hair. He yelled across the street.

"Are you calling the devil?"

The woman hesitated for a moment. Should she answer? At first, she was on guard, but her curiosity won out. Who was that stranger who looked like he didn't belong in this middle-class neighborhood? He wore baggy, below-the-waist dirty jeans and an old brown leather jacket, but no hat and gloves in spite of the January cold. His unkempt dark hair and long, salt-and-pepper beard were waving in the wind. On his back, he carried a sleeping bag on top of a backpack. He looked like a drifter. However, his demeanor inspired trust, so the woman decided that it was safe to answer from the other side of the street.

"No, it's my cat's name." She paused for a moment. "It used to be my own name," she added mischievously.

"Really? Cool name! Who chose it? Your parents?"

Somehow, she felt like giving him a truthful answer. Usually she was evasive in answering questions about her name, taking malicious pleasure in keeping people hanging. But this man seemed genuinely interested in a real answer.

"No, I chose the name Devil for myself when I was a teenager. My parents named me Daisy at birth. But I got tired of people forgetting which flower I was. Rose? Violet? Daisy? Once, someone even called me Pansy."

"Funny!"

"That's when I decided to change my name. At first I thought of June. It happens to be my favorite month of the year. Then I realized people might confuse June with May or call me something else having to do with the time of year, like Autumn, so I chose the name Devil."

"Why?"

"I liked it because it fit my personality as a rebellious teenager. But my husband hated that name. He discovered by glancing at my driver's license that my official first name was Daisy, and he started calling me Dizzy Daisy. It became Dizzy after a while. That's my name now."

"I like it!"

Sam obviously wanted to keep the conversation going. "Tell me, are you a native of Oregon?"

"No. I was born and grew up on the East Coast. I came here for college. My parents were against it, but I managed to get a scholarship, so they let me go. I really wanted to leave New England. People are so stuffy there! I was a rebel."

"That's why you chose the name Devil for yourself!"

"Yeah, and now it's my cat's name. I got him after my husband died. He's an orange cat, and he's really a devil."

After a while, Dizzy felt like sharing her sad story with the stranger. He seemed to have all the time in the world to listen to her.

"I'm looking for my cat, he's lost. It's my fault. I should've known better. I went out of town for two days and a friend of mine offered to take care of Devil. I forgot to tell her that he's an indoor cat. Maggie must've left the front door open and my cat ran away. When I returned yesterday, Devil was nowhere to be seen." She paused for a while. "I made a mistake. I should've warned my friend. My husband was right to call me Dizzy, I'm silly."

She burst into youthful laughter. Sam was really intrigued by this elderly lady who was able to laugh at herself.

"You sure sound happy."

"Better laugh than cry!"

"Tell me, can I help you find your cat?"

Dizzy stared at him from across the street. He was a middle-aged man, at least half her age, with a disheveled look, probably homeless. She crossed the street to take a closer look. He smelled like he hadn't showered for a long time. But it was tempting to accept his offer to help look for Devil.

"What's your name?"

"Sam."

He noticed her inquisitive look.

"I know I'm dirty and smelly. Homeless just now. I slept under a bridge all of last week. They have no shower there."

"Why don't you go to a homeless shelter?"

"I have, but last week the place was full every evening. It's winter, you know. I should've gone earlier in the day, but I forget the time fooling around on my harmonica."

"So you're a musician?"

"Sort of. I used to wait tables in a bar and sometimes I played a song on my guitar. People liked it and gave me good tips. It encouraged me to keep playing. But I don't have a job at that bar now. It was forced to close down."

"Why?"

"Oh, some fussy neighbors complained to the police about the noise. Sure got noisy when the customers were drunk." He paused. "I never found a job like that after the bar closed down."

"What kind of work?"

"Any kind, as long as the job's in a funky place."

"How long have you tried?"

"A few months."

"Do you get unemployment just now?"

"No." He continued with pride in his voice and whole demeanor. "I don't want to deal with that stupid bureaucracy. I'd rather be poor but free."

"So you're a rebel too."

"Yeah, you've got it! My dad was one of those bureaucrats. He sent me to college. I was there for two years."

"That's why you can speak so well when you want to. You learned it in college."

"Maybe, but I always wanted to escape that prison. It was too uptight for me. My dad's dead now. He wasted his whole life. My mother…" Sam choked up, obviously emotional at the thought of her. "My mother's like you and me. She's a rebel! I see her once in a while. Last time we visited, she told me that she'd tried to get a waitress job, but they wanted someone younger."

"How old is she?"

"Around seventy."

"That's not so old." Sam looked at her in disbelief.

"Seventy isn't that old to you? You must be older."

"I'm eighty."

"You're kidding. You're like my mother. When she had me, she was thirty. People thought she was twenty. Now she looks like she's sixty. She tried to fool people in the interview for that job, but they looked at her papers. She told me she left the place screaming and slamming the door." Sam looked at Dizzy. "You sounded like a young girl when you were calling your cat earlier."

"I'm a happy person. But today I'm pretending. I'm sad because my cat's missing. He's such good company for me!"

"Let me help you find Devil."

"You remembered my cat's name!"

"Yeah, that's what two years of college did for me, training my memory. So much rote learning in classes like botany…"

"You know botany! Good! I bet you can tell me the name of a bush I saw on the next block the other day."

"Let's go look. You lead the way."

Dizzy was hesitant. She had been living in her rental house only two weeks, after selling the family home a few blocks away. What would her new neighbors think if they saw her walking with a disheveled man much younger than she was? She calculated in her head: *If Sam's mother was around seventy and she was thirty when her son was born, he must be about forty years old, half her age.* She turned her head and spoke under her breath so Sam couldn't hear.

"I don't care what the neighbors might think."

"What did you say?"

"Nothing. Let's go. I'll show you that bush."

Sam followed her, carrying his possessions on his back. When they reached the front yard where the bush was, Dizzy pointed it out to him. He put down his backpack and sleeping bag on the sidewalk and carefully inspected the bush.

"That's a *Grevillea victoriae.*"

"You know the scientific name!"

"I didn't mean to show off. Let's call it a winter-blooming plant. People like the red-orange flowers. It's something cheerful before the spring flowers."

"Thank you, I was curious." She paused for a minute. "You speak especially well when you talk about plants. And you sure know a lot about botany."

"That's one class I didn't hate. Except the quizzes and exams of course. At least it was about real things." He reflected for a moment. "Do you want to see other winter-blooming flowers? I know a park in town that has lots of them." Dizzy pretended not to have heard his last remarks and returned to the topic of her cat.

"Shall we look for Devil? Where could he be?"

"If he's an indoor cat, he can't have gone very far."

"Right! Let's look around here. Poor Devil doesn't know how to cope with the outdoors."

"You sound like a real animal lover."

"Sure. I used to have a dog. His name was Whiskey, but he died last year."

"Poor Whiskey!"

"Now I prefer cats."

"Why?"

"Because cats are so curious, like me. Curiosity is what keeps me going."

They started walking along the winding streets of her neighborhood. Suddenly, he dropped his backpack and sleeping bag on the sidewalk.

"I'm starved, haven't eaten since last night. Let's see what I have in here."

He sat down and pulled out a moldy piece of cheddar cheese and a few slices of old bread. He offered them to Dizzy.

"Would you like some?"

"No, thanks, I already had lunch."

He sensed that she was lying but said nothing. *Maybe this lady was a snob after all.*

"Are you thirsty?"

"Yes, a little bit."

"All I have is whiskey." He pulled out a half-full bottle. "Someone gave it to me yesterday, a man I knew at the bar. Had half of it last night. It's really strong stuff. Do you want to try it?"

"No, thanks, I only drink in the evening. A glass of red wine with my dinner."

"Got it! You don't want to drink out of the bottle. Snobs like to drink out of a glass."

Dizzy was piqued by Sam's remark. She grabbed the bottle and swallowed a shot, just to show him she wasn't a snob. She immediately felt so tipsy that she had to sit down on the sidewalk. Sam was slowly eating his bread and cheese.

"I'm getting drunk," she said.

"Have some bread and cheese."

This time Dizzy told no white lies, hoping that food would make her feel better. Sam handed her some of his old bread and moldy cheese, and she gulped them down. The food did her some good, but she was feeling very tired, so she lay down on the sidewalk, having lost all self-consciousness and sense of decorum. A man she occasionally had seen in the neighborhood walked by and glanced at her with a disapproving look. She didn't care.

Sam became concerned when he noticed she was shivering in the cool winter air. "Are you cold, Dizzy? Let me help you." He covered her carefully with his dirty sleeping bag. Then he pulled his harmonica out of his backpack and started playing a song. She was all ears.

"What's that tune? I don't recognize it."

"I just made it up."

"So you're a composer?"

"Sort of, I just get inspired and start playing."

Dizzy became reflective. She had thought of herself as an imaginative person, but this stranger beat her; he was so creative!

"Can you play a song on your guitar?"

"No, I sold it just before Christmas. Got a harmonica instead."

"Why?"

"It's good to have very few possessions, and light. That way, you're free to travel."

*****

A few minutes later, a lady came out of a nearby house with her dog on a leash. The dog, a cute small poodle, barked at the sight of someone lying on the sidewalk. Dizzy stood up and remembered that she was looking for Devil. She addressed the lady.

"Have you by any chance seen an orange cat looking lost?"

"No. How did you lose him?"

"He ran away from my house."

"So you're looking for your cat, you and your husband…"

"He's not my husband. He's a man I just met on the street."

The lady immediately retreated, pulling on the leash to get her little dog away from Sam's sleeping bag.

"Come on, sweetie, let's go home. I forgot to turn off the stove." She turned to Dizzy and Sam. "Good luck to you. I hope you find your cat."

After the lady and her dog left hurriedly, Dizzy noticed a few wet spots on the sidewalk.

"Look, Sam, the dog peed a little bit on your sleeping bag. That must be why that lady left in a big hurry. I'm sorry."

"Don't worry. The dog was marking his territory, close to his home. That's normal."

"You're so forgiving!"

"I really love animals." He paused. "Let's go look for Devil, if you're rested."

Sam picked up his backpack and put it on his back again. Dizzy helped him roll up his sleeping bag and fit it on top of his backpack.

11

They proceeded along the sidewalk, calling Devil once in a while and hoping to hear a *meow* in response.

*****

Sam and Dizzy started climbing a steep street. Suddenly a car sped down the hill. The driver apparently didn't notice an animal crossing the street. It was a cat. The speeding car killed the animal, but the driver didn't stop. A young couple came out of a house, and the woman screamed in horror.

"That's my cat!"

Dizzy burst into tears, thinking that it could have been Devil. She addressed the young woman.

"Can I do anything for you?"

"No! It's too late!" She turned to the man next to her. "I told you not to leave the door open."

"I didn't, you did!"

They started arguing loudly. Dizzy felt uncomfortable and wanted to leave. Anyway, there was nothing she could do. She turned to Sam.

"I'm exhausted. Plus, it's going to get dark pretty soon. Let's go to my house and have something to eat."

"OK, no more old bread and moldy cheese for you."

"And especially no more whiskey."

"Out of the bottle…"

"Are you making fun of me?"

"Couldn't resist the joke. Anyway, you want normal food."

Dizzy was piqued again. She concocted a weird menu in her head, so that the stranger would be in for a surprise. They walked in silence for a few minutes. When they got to the top of the hill, she was out of breath. Sam offered his arm to her. She resisted.

"I may be an old lady, but I climb that hill every day with no help. Today it's different. I feel tired because my cat is missing."

"Maybe Devil is hiding in your house. Let me look. I'm a good finder."

She kept quiet, wondering if Sam was looking for a place to crash overnight. In that case, she decided she would have to call the cops, which she hated to do.

"What are you thinking, Dizzy?"

"I'm thinking of what food I have at home."

"It's going to be cold tonight. After we eat I'll go to the men's shelter. Want to see if they have a place for me." Dizzy felt relieved that he was considering the homeless shelter.

*****

They finally reached Dizzy's house and she opened the door. Sam was utterly surprised to see the almost empty living room. There was no furniture except a computer desk by a window and a music system in a corner of the room. Nothing on the walls. It looked bare.

"Dizzy, you have no furniture!"

"Oh, I'm a minimalist, especially now. Why keep things at my age? My husband was a pack rat. After he died, I decided to downsize a lot. But I wanted to keep my computer and my music system. I use them a lot. Plus, one chair and a small table in the kitchen." She laughed. "I love sitting on the floor in the living room. It reminds me of being a teenager when I used to listen to jazz and pop music for hours." She turned to Sam. "Will you be uncomfortable sitting on the floor to eat?"

"Are you kidding? I'm used to it. But I thought for sure a lady like you have nice furniture."

"I used to. No regrets about getting rid of it. It's like getting rid of your past. It's liberating."

"You're a strange lady!"

Dizzy went to the kitchen, and he followed her. She opened the fridge and pulled out of the vegetable drawer some carrot and celery sticks. She also found a few strawberries and a container of garlic hummus.

"Will that be enough for you, Sam? Oh, I also have some red wine…"

"And glasses?" he asked teasingly. She burst out laughing.

"No, I gave them away. I only kept one for myself. If you don't want to drink out of the bottle, we can share the glass."

"Whatever…You're cool for your age." She laughed again while uncorking the bottle of wine. "At least I kept a corkscrew." She opened a cabinet that was almost empty. "I gave away most of my real plates, so we'll use paper plates."

"No problem. I usually have no plate at all."

"I feel so light, having almost no furniture in the living room and only essentials in the kitchen. My bedroom is another story. It's full of things."

"Can I see?"

Dizzy bit her tongue and found a quick excuse not to show the stranger her bedroom. "Oh, it's a mess in there. I kept all kinds of things that are memories of my husband or relatives and friends. Each one has the name of the person who gave it to me. I cherish those things. So many emotions attached to them…"

"Of course!"

For a moment they both were silent, Dizzy reflecting on her past and people who had been close to her. Then she broke the silence, returning to the present. "I poured some wine in the glass and the feast is ready. Let's sit down before it gets cold." She giggled at her own joke. "You have first dibs on the wine."

"OK." He drank out of the single glass and smacked his lips. "You have good taste. This is really good wine."

"Have some veggies and fruit!" They ate the vegetable sticks and strawberries, taking turns to drink wine out of the only glass.

"Sam, can I ask you another question about plants?"

"Go ahead."

"What's the name of the white flowers that smell like vanilla?"

"With dark green foliage?"

"I don't know. I didn't pay attention to the foliage. The flowers were so beautiful…"

"I'd have to see the foliage. Where did you see that plant?"

"In a park at the other end of town. I think it's called Pleasant Park."

"That one! I know it very well. Last summer I slept there almost every night. How about showing me the plant in the park?"

Dizzy was hesitant to commit; it was too fast for her. After all, Sam was a homeless stranger. She gave an excuse that she thought was brilliant. "I don't have a car any longer. Now I depend on city buses."

"Like me. Let's meet at the entrance of the park. There's a bus stop right by the park. Tomorrow…"

"No, tomorrow I have to look for my cat."

"All day?"

"Yes. I want to knock on doors in the neighborhood. Someone might have taken Devil in."

"Maybe." He reflected for a while. "You want to go to the park the next day? I'll come and get you. We can ride the bus together."

"OK. Come on Wednesday at one o'clock."

"See you the day after tomorrow." He stood up, picked up his backpack and sleeping bag, adjusted them on his back, and left without saying goodbye.

*****

After Sam had gone, Dizzy was relieved that she didn't have to call the cops after all. At the same time, she felt a little guilty about not revealing to the homeless man the existence of an empty spare bedroom in her house. *Oh well*, she figured, *he would probably go back to his usual sleeping place under the bridge if the shelter was full again.*

While picking up the empty paper plates from the living room floor, she reflected for a moment. Should she have agreed to go to the park with a stranger, even if he knew about plants? But was Sam a stranger? Or was he a providential new friend, at a time when she felt somewhat lonely, because she recently had moved to a new house and her cat was missing?

She quickly dismissed the thought of an enduring friendship with a homeless man who was half her age, also recalling how dirty

15

and smelly he was. Anyway, her main preoccupation right now was Devil. Where could her cat have gone?

Dizzy decided to listen to some music in order to lessen her anxiety about her missing cat. One day at a time! Hopefully, tomorrow she would find him. She grabbed a CD set of piano music by Satie and started listening to *Le Piccadilly*, a music-hall piece that was inspired by Scott Joplin's ragtime music. While dancing barefoot in her living room, the elderly lady flashed back to a quote from Satie that showed his humorous take on music.

> That art has done me more harm than good, really: it has made me quarrel with people of quality, most honorable, more-than-distinguished, terribly genteel people.

Dizzy also remembered that long ago in a piano performance class. She had tried to play with her teacher a four-hand piece by Satie called *Three pieces in the shape of a pear*. The title had intrigued her. A few months later, she had found out that the composer named his piece that way in response to a comment by Claude Debussy. This rival musician had once said that Satie's compositions had "no form." The humorous composer had responded by creating an unconventional piece with a flippant title. Satie's tongue-in-cheek humor made Dizzy feel joyful.

She played one more CD of Satie's compositions called *Danses gothiques* as a way to calm her mind about her missing cat. Then she went to bed early. Gone were her usual sweet dreams, however. Instead, she had nightmares about Devil being run over by a speeding car. She was really anxious about her beloved cat.

CHAPTER 2

"Devil! Devil!"

Dizzy's voice broke the silence of the early morning. She had gone out at seven o'clock, after her agitated night full of nightmares about her cat. Now she walked briskly down the sidewalk. She skipped the first house since all the shades were still down, a sign that her new next-door neighbors must still be asleep.

As she reached the end of the block without knocking on any door at that early hour, an elderly man came out of his house. "What are you doing? It's only seven o'clock. It's still dark. And here you are, waking up the whole neighborhood!"

"I lost my cat. His name is Devil and I was calling him. I wish he would answer. Have you seen him by any chance?"

"There are so many cats around here."

"He's an orange cat and very pretty."

"That's what *you* say!"

"But it's true. He's medium size…"

The man had gone back inside, angrily slamming his front door. Dizzy crossed the street, hoping to find nicer people. Her wish was granted. On the other side of the street, two blocks down, a lovely young woman came out of a modest house with a baby sleeping in her arms.

"I heard you calling Devil. Have you lost your cat?"

"How did you know that Devil is a cat?"

"Oh, I used to have one called the same. He was black and white, a really nice cat." She started to cry. "But he got run over by a car last summer. I still miss him."

"I'm sorry…Do you have another cat now?" Dizzy asked in a soothing tone of voice.

"Not just now. Soon after he died, I got pregnant and my husband told me I'd be very busy with the baby for a while."

"What's your baby's name?"

"Daffodil. My husband and I like flowers, so we chose that name for our first child."

"Nice name! My parents liked flowers too, so they named me Daisy, but now I go by Dizzy."

"That's a funny name!"

"I like it because people don't forget it, especially when they see how silly I can be."

Cindy looked at the elderly lady. "You aren't silly. You're just playful, I guess." She paused for a minute. "Are you new in the neighborhood?"

"Yes and no. I just moved to a new house a few blocks from my old place."

"Let's get acquainted. Do you want to come in? I have coffee ready in the kitchen. It's good to have a hot drink on a cold January morning."

"Thank you, but I'll pass this time. I want to walk around the whole neighborhood before people go to work. I'll start knocking on doors pretty soon. Maybe somebody took my Devil in."

"Up to you. But now that we met, why don't you drop in one of these days? We're close neighbors. Next time you can see my baby when she's awake. She usually wakes up around eight o'clock."

"OK. What's your name?"

"Cindy."

"See you later, Cindy."

Dizzy felt good about having met a nice neighbor a few blocks from her house, especially after encountering the grouchy old man closer to her place. She resumed her walk, calling Devil once in a while. On the next block, she noticed a couple walking their dogs and followed them until she caught up with them. She addressed them both.

"Good morning!"

The man and the woman stopped and turned to greet her.

"Good morning!"

"You look familiar. Do you live around here?" asked Dizzy. "I just moved at the top of the hill. I think I've seen you walking your dogs in the neighborhood."

"That's possible! My husband and I walk our dogs twice a day. We're both retired, so we have time." She paused. "You look familiar too. Don't you walk around here too?"

"That's right, I take a walk every day, rain or shine. This morning I'm looking for my cat. I lost him."

"Maybe we can help you find him. What's his name?"

"Devil. He's an orange cat. Have you seen him?"

"No, but let's look together. He's probably hiding somewhere."

Dizzy led the way, followed by the couple and their three black dogs. The woman was handling one, and the man had two of them on a single leash. Every time the two dogs pulled on the leash to explore some bushes on a front lawn, the elderly lady hoped that they had discovered her cat's hideout but in vain. When they reached a big white house, all three dogs got very excited and marked their territory. Dizzy, who was ahead of them, stopped and turned to the woman.

"I guess this is your house. Thank you for trying to help me."

"I'm sorry we didn't find your cat. Would you like to come in and have a cup of coffee?"

"No, thank you. Another day, maybe. Today I want to keep looking for my cat."

"I understand. Let us know when you find him. Here's our phone number."

The woman pulled out of her coat pocket a business card with their names, John and Daisy Swift. The lady's first name evoked memories for Dizzy, but she refrained from telling her long story. She left and continued her search for Devil.

*****

After an hour walking around the neighborhood and knocking on some doors, she felt exhausted and decided to go home and take

19

a nap. Once at home, she fell asleep immediately and had a strange dream.

She was downtown one morning and saw a man that looked like Sam. He recognized her and told her that he was going on a five-mile hike. Did she want to join him? She accepted his offer, and they walked together through town toward the surrounding woods. At the bottom of the hills, she lost sight of him and decided to explore this remote part of the town that she didn't know. She was curious.

In her dream, Dizzy was relieved to reach a commercial neighborhood where she might get a refreshing drink. Obviously it was a Spanish-speaking neighborhood. She saw a store named *Azteca* that exhibited colorful serapes in the window. Forgetting about her thirst, she entered the store and was attracted to a baby clothing section. It gave her the idea of getting a present for that lovely young neighbor with the baby girl named Daffodil.

Rummaging through the baby items, the first thing Dizzy picked was an adorable blue crocheted hat. She liked the fact that it had been made by hand but rejected it for its color; blue wasn't an appropriate color for a baby girl. She looked in vain for a pink one. However, she found a yellow one. It was so cute that she decided to buy it.

When she awoke from her nap, Dizzy was ready to act immediately on her dream, hoping to forget her grief about her missing cat. She decided to get a present for the baby that afternoon and visit that lovely neighbor early the next morning. She remembered that Sam wasn't due that day until one o'clock.

After a light lunch, sitting on the single chair in her kitchen, Dizzy caught a city bus and went downtown to buy a present for Daffodil. As in her dream, she found a cute yellow hat and bought it, hoping that the color would not offend the mother. She returned home on the city bus and wrapped the present in colorful paper.

*****

The next morning around eight o'clock, she walked to Cindy's house, looking again for Devil on the way. When she reached her destination, she rang the bell. Cindy appeared at the door and greeted her cheerfully.

"Good morning! I was hoping to see you again today. Come in and meet my baby. She's awake this time."

"Good morning, Daffodil. I brought you a little present. I'd better give it to your mother."

"You didn't have to do that."

"But I wanted to."

Dizzy handed Cindy the wrapped present, anxiously awaiting the mother's reaction.

"Oh, how cute. I love yellow. That's one reason we named our baby Daffodil."

"I noticed she was dressed in yellow yesterday."

"I didn't want to conform: blue for boys, pink for girls."

"I'm a lot older than you, but we seem to look at things the same way."

"We can be friends from now on. Never mind the age difference. Come by as often as you want. We can chat over coffee. By the way, would you like a cup of fresh coffee? I made it two hours ago for my husband."

"He goes to work early?"

"Yes, and it gets lonely before Daffodil wakes up. Then I get really busy with her all morning." She looked at her baby. "Daffodil just woke up, so I'll give her a few minutes to rest. Then she'll want to be fed..."

"You're nursing her?"

"Of course. It's so healthy for her and it makes me feel good too! Can I nurse her in front of you?"

"Go right ahead. I'm not a Puritan. In the past, we had to hide under a blanket to nurse a baby. One time I forgot to cover myself when breastfeeding in public, and my own husband was so embarrassed!" She paused. "I feel so free now as a widow! My kids and older grandkids think I'm too carefree, but one has to live it up and enjoy life!"

"I like your attitude." After a while, Cindy asked hesitantly. "Do you see your kids and grandkids very often?"

"No, they are so busy! Anyway, two of my kids and their families live far away. I've got one son in town. But I only see him and his wife once in a while. They call me when they need childcare for their daughter. I'm happy to do it for them, because this way I get to see my granddaughter. She's six now. I especially loved taking care of her when she was a baby."

"I wish my mom would be like you! She won't babysit for me."

"Why?"

"She says she's done enough in the past. Before my dad died, she was a slave. He was very demanding."

"Just like my husband. Now I live as a free spirit."

"Good for you!"

"By the way, I'd love to babysit Daffodil when you and your husband want to go out in the evening."

"You really wouldn't mind?"

"Not at all. I love babies. And, believe me, I know how to change diapers."

"You're a great lady!"

Cindy poured coffee into a cup and handed it to her guest, who drank it. Then Dizzy looked at the clock and got up from her chair.

"Already eight twenty. Today I can't stay. I've got to look for Devil. But I'll come back some other day after I find him. Bye-bye, Cindy and Daffodil. See you soon!"

"Goodbye, my new friend, and thanks for the present."

*****

Dizzy left precipitously and continued her search for Devil, calling him once in a while. At the bottom of the hill, she saw a lady and a little boy come out of their pink house. The lady was speaking a mixture of French and English.

"*Depêche-toi*, Marc! Hurry up!"

"Mom, I am *depêche-toi*-ing."

"I told you many times that it's bad to mix English and French in the same word."

"I can't help it. You confuse me. You should just speak English, like everybody else here."

"I can speak the way I want. Come, we will be late for school."

The mother grabbed the little boy's hand and they started walking hurriedly toward the elementary school. Dizzy caught up with them and asked in broken French if they'd seen an orange cat around. The lady spoke in English to her.

"Ah, you speak French…"

"Just a little bit. It's easier in English." She turned to the little boy. "I've lost my orange cat. Have you seen him?"

"What's his name?"

"Devil."

"'Cool! But we haven't seen a cat looking lost, right, Mom?"

"No. Come, Marc, we will be late for school," she said impatiently.

Dizzy was disappointed. She kept looking for her cat in front yards on the next block. A few minutes later, she met the mother again, and they engaged in a conversation.

"Excuse me for being *pressée*, *euh*, in a hurry earlier. Now that my son is in school, I would like to talk to you."

"To me? In English, please."

"Let me ask you a question. Do you enjoy walking?"

"Yeah, very much."

"I am looking for someone to take my son to school and back home." She sounded like she had rehearsed her request in English. "My job is at the other end of town. It is hard for me to give him rides. Anyway, it is good for him to walk to school. It is so close to our home! But he is too young to go by himself."

"How old is he?"

"Seven."

Dizzy thought to herself that the mother was too protective and that her seven-year-old son could safely walk by himself in this middle-class neighborhood, but she kept quiet. Then the French lady made a surprising proposal to her.

"Would you be free to take him to school in the morning and back home after school?"

"But you don't know me."

"I know many people around here. I told some of them that I was looking for childcare. They told me about you, and by chance you and I met on the street. I knew it was you…"

"Because of my weird looks?"

"Anyway, the people around here say that you are very reliable… in spite of your strange ways since the death of your husband." She became business-like. "Can you come in the late afternoon to discuss things?"

"Not today, I'm looking for my cat." Dizzy avoided telling the French lady that Sam was due at her home in the afternoon.

"I understand. Then can you come and see me on Saturday morning at nine o'clock? We could talk over coffee about the exact schedule and the pay."

"You mean, you'll pay me?"

"Of course. It is a job."

"But I'm old…"

"No problem! Age means nothing to me, as long as I can trust you."

"Good!"

"We live in the pink house on the next block.

"I know. I saw you and your son coming out of that house earlier. See you on Saturday morning."

"See you *samedi*, I mean Saturday."

Dizzy went on looking for Devil. She was sad about having lost him but happy about having met nice people in the neighborhood. A sense of community overcame her. Before her husband's death, she was so busy at home and on her daytime nursing job that she had no time to get to know people around her home. Now that she had moved to a house a few blocks away, she enjoyed the thought of having met new neighbors because of her missing cat.

*****

As Dizzy walked, she reflected on her past life. Suddenly she heard two people arguing loudly on their front porch. She recognized the voices of the young couple whose cat had been recently killed by a car. The woman was screaming.

"You don't even care what happens to me. You are so insensitive! I've decided I don't want to live with you anymore, Dan."

"Look, Vivian, I know you're upset about Mimi. It's too bad that she got run over by a car. But she was just a cat."

"How can you say that? She was my daughter!"

"Your daughter? Don't you think your love for cats is too extreme?"

"Too extreme? What do you mean?"

"You seem to care more for pets than for people."

"I happen to like both pets and people. What's wrong with that?"

Dizzy felt like agreeing with Vivian but refrained from interfering. She just asked the two of them if they had seen an orange cat looking lost.

"Dan, is that the cat we saw a while ago on our front lawn?"

"No, Vivian, that cat was grey."

"I could swear it was orange."

"You're wrong, Vivian. I'm sure it was gray."

"You're right. It was the neighbors' cat from across the street."

At that point, Dizzy left hurriedly. She was afraid the couple would start arguing again and wanted no part of it. She felt like being home on her own. No more searching for Devil just now. Maybe he would come back miraculously! Besides, Sam was due at one o'clock that afternoon.

CHAPTER 3

When Dizzy reached her house, she was hungry and decided to have an early lunch. As she stood by the kitchen counter, eating an avocado sandwich on a napkin and drinking tomato juice from the only cup she owned, she wondered whether Sam would show up as promised.

At exactly one o'clock, her doorbell rang. She rushed to open the front door. A nice-looking man stood on the steps, dressed in black trousers and a light brown leather jacket. She stood there, perplexed.

"Hello, Dizzy, don't you recognize me? I'm Sam."

"Oh, you look so different!"

"I got dressed up for you today. I went to the Salvation Army and got this outfit. Not bad, eh?"

"You didn't have to do that. We're only going to a park."

"But your botany teacher wanted to look decent. Besides, it might make me talk like a gentleman on a date."

Dizzy got concerned. Was the park expedition some kind of date? Was Sam using his knowledge of plants as a way to get closer to her than she wanted? What were his intentions? Should she cancel the park expedition? *Nonsense*, she told herself, *he couldn't be interested in romance with me. He's half my age.* She silently grabbed her winter jacket, scarf, hat, and gloves and put them on.

"I'm almost ready to go, Sam. Have you eaten lunch?"

"Lunch can wait. I checked the schedule, and the bus is due in a few minutes."

"Let me tie my shoes. Once I forgot to tie my shoes, silly me. One lace caught in the front door, and I fell headfirst on the pavement..."

"Hurry up! You can tell me your stories later."

"Should I take an umbrella?"

"And the kitchen sink?" He chuckled. "Come on. We can't miss the bus. It should be here any time now. Lock your door and let's go."

"I don't need to lock my door."

"That's right. You've got so little to steal."

"Anyway, if I ever get burglarized, I'll think the burglars needed what they stole more than I do."

"Even if they stole your computer or your music system?"

"I can replace them."

"What about the things in your bedroom you were telling me about?"

"You probably think I have valuables in there. Not really, but you're right. I'm attached to souvenirs that remind me of people in my long life." She sighed and then laughed. "I figure burglars are mostly after valuables. When they see how bare my living room is, they'll give up and leave."

"You're a smart lady!"

Dizzy liked Sam's compliment. After she finished tying her shoes, they rushed to the bus stop two blocks away. Alas, the bus had already come and gone.

"We missed it, Sam. It's my fault. I take so long to get ready in the winter."

"And you were about to take an umbrella."

"Don't chide me. It makes me feel like a little girl! But what shall we do now?"

"That bus only runs every hour. It'll be too late for the park. Days are very short in January."

"I have an idea. Some of my neighbors are great gardeners, and they take especially good care of their front yards. Why don't we take a walk like we did the other day and look at their winter gardens? You could teach me the names of the plants, and we can keep looking for my cat too."

"Cool! Kill two birds with one stone."

"Please don't use that expression, Sam. It makes me think that Devil might have escaped to look for birds."

"And kill them?"

"I tried to train him not to do that. One day, before I decided to keep him indoors, Devil came home triumphantly carrying a dead bird in his mouth. I punished him."

"Shame on you. That's instinct for cats."

"I know. But don't play moralist with me!"

"OK, I'll say no more."

They started slowly retracing their steps, catching their breath after their mad race for the bus. Dizzy felt relieved that Sam was looking more decent than he did a couple of days ago. He had even combed his wild hair and trimmed his beard.

They entered her house for a short rest and a light lunch for Sam. Dizzy offered him assorted veggie sticks and a glass of milk. He accepted them and went to sit on the floor by the window in the living room. She joined him carrying a paper cup that she had filled from the kitchen faucet for herself. While quenching her thirst, she was internally rehearsing her answer, in case any neighbors were in their front yards and nosy enough to ask about Sam. She would tell them he was her nephew. It was only a white lie.

"Look, Dizzy, some winter jasmine in the yard across the street. I can see it through the window."

"You mean these bright yellow flowers? I noticed them when I moved here."

"Yeah, they come and go all winter."

"The color is pretty. But one day I tried to smell them. No fragrance at all!"

"True, like cyclamens. If you like to smell plants, you must be happy that winter sweet is in full bloom this month. Its yellow flowers have a really sweet fragrance!"

"Sam, I find your speech so different when you talk about plants! You sound like a college teacher."

"I know. Maybe I shouldn't have dropped out of college. By now I'd be teaching botany, instead of being homeless."

"It's never too late to go back to college and get a degree."

"Too late for me. By now I'm used to my free lifestyle and all the bad stuff that comes with it." He kept silent for a minute and changed the topic. "Dizzy, look at this sweet box in your next-door neighbor's yard. It's about to bloom. No spectacular flowers, but you'll like the fragrance."

"I like both colorful flowers and fragrance."

"You're a spoiled woman. You want everything in life!"

"Why not? Life has to be enjoyed." She paused. "Sam, do you like yellow flowers? I like that color, especially. It brings me joy."

"Then you should enjoy forsythia when it blooms in early spring. It has bright yellow flowers."

"I also like crocuses of different colors because they announce spring. But my favorite of all flowers is the poppies that come later."

"You like poppies? Is that because some kinds of poppies are sources of opium?"

"Stop teasing me, Sam. Do I look like a drug addict?"

"You never know. Some people hide their addiction very well."

"You should speak for yourself! Are you a drug addict? Is that why you live on the streets?"

"Stop it! It's getting too personal."

"You're right. I'll keep quiet." She changed the topic. "Let's go for our walk. I've got some questions for you about the flowers in my next-door neighbors' front yard."

Out they went, first stopping to admire the garden next door. As they were trying to get close to a winter sweet bush, an elderly man came out of the house and addressed them in an angry tone of voice.

"What are you doing in my garden? This is private property!"

"We only wanted to smell the flowers, right, Sam?"

"Who is this Sam?"

"A nephew of mine who's visiting for a few days from Chicago. By the way, I'm your new next-door neighbor."

"I know. Two weeks ago, we saw you move in. Are you renting the place?"

"Yes, for now. My husband died last summer, and I just sold our big house a few blocks away. It was too much work for me, so I decided to downsize a lot."

"That's why you came with only a small truckload. My wife and I were wondering…"

"You have a wife. Can I meet her?"

"No, she's really sick. In a wheelchair. She doesn't come out anymore. Cancer of the liver. I'm her caregiver now."

"I'm so sorry!"

Dizzy felt bad that she and Sam had intruded on a man who was taking care of his sick wife, no matter how rude he had been at first. She asked if she could help. Receiving no answer from her grumpy next-door neighbor, she said goodbye and pulled Sam away from the winter sweet bush that he was contemplating.

They continued their walk, admiring plants and calling Devil every once in a while. However, her lost cat was nowhere to be seen.

"Sam, the other day you bragged about being a good finder. Later, will you look again for my cat all around the house, including my bedroom this time? Maybe he's hiding somewhere inside."

"Too late! He'd have come out from his hiding place when he heard you. Cats get hungry, like everyone else, and want to be fed. It's more likely that someone took him in. Or he could be lost in the woods and never come back."

Dizzy burst into tears. Sam felt bad about suggesting Devil could be lost forever. He thought of a new topic of conversation.

"I can see you love flowers. Have you been to the desert in early spring? The flowers are fantastic then."

"My husband used to go every year to the desert, mostly in California. Sometimes I went with him. Once we went to Joshua Tree in Arizona. We stayed at a motel for four days and went hiking every day in the desert. The ocotillo trees were in full bloom. I loved it! But my husband is gone now."

"Can't you go to the desert by yourself?"

"It wouldn't be that much fun, and I can't drive that far by myself." (Pensively) "My husband was good company on trips. Not at other times."

"What do you mean?"

"He was a tyrant. Wanted me to stay home with him and the kids when I wasn't at work."

"How many kids do you have?"

"Three. Two boys and one girl."

"Apparently you didn't like being a wife and mother."

"I liked it, but it wasn't enough for me. I also wanted to be out in the world, for example, getting more educated."

"And your husband didn't let you?"

"He said it was OK. But when I started going to college to get a degree in art history, he got jealous…"

"Really? What did he do?"

"He tried everything to make me fail. He would pretend to need me at home." Dizzy continued spilling out to Sam. "Once he had promised me to take the day off at work and watch the kids. They were small then, and I had an exam that day." She continued in an angry tone of voice. "At the last minute, my husband said his boss needed him for some business. I wasn't able to take the exam that day, and later I got kicked out of the program. It was my husband's fault."

"What a fool!"

"Don't talk about my husband that way!"

"You loved him?"

"In a way, because he respected my need for solitude when I wasn't busy at home." She caught her breath. "But let me finish my long story. After that miserable day when I missed the exam, I decided to forget about studying art history and use my nursing degree. I got a job as a nurse in a hospital."

"And your husband liked that?"

"Yeah, because he was much older than me, and he thought I might become his caregiver someday. He was happy that I learned a lot, working at the hospital."

"How long did you work there?

"For thirty years. When they wanted me to retire at age sixty, I became a private nurse until my husband's death last summer."

"You must enjoy having more time for yourself now."

"Yes. It was hard being a married woman and working full time as a nurse."

"Why did you work so hard? Your husband didn't make enough money?"

"It was a tight budget, with three kids. Besides, I frankly needed to recharge my batteries when I got depressed at home. Especially when the kids left the nest one by one, and my husband got sick in the last years of his life."

Dizzy became pensive and shed a few tears. Then she turned to Sam.

"Enough of that. I must bore you with my sad tales. Why don't we talk more about desert flowers? I'd love to go on trips again, but I don't have a car anymore."

"You used to have a car?"

"It was a family car."

"What did you with it?"

"I sold it after my husband died."

"'Cause you needed the money?"

"Not really, but I'm getting old and my vision isn't that good for driving anymore."

"I could be your driver."

"Really? We could go to the desert together?"

She regretted her impulsive question and kept quiet for a while. He broke the silence.

"We would need a car."

"I could buy a used car." She reflected for a few minutes. "I just got some money from the sale of our big house. It's silly to keep it in the bank, with interest rates so low right now!"

"Dizzy, you're a sharp businesswoman."

"You have to be, especially when you're a widow. But I'm no genius when it comes to mechanics. Could you help me find a reliable used car?"

"How about looking together this weekend?"

"That's a great idea! I'd love to go to the desert soon, if you can be the driver."

"Let me tell you, I love to drive. Used to have an old jalopy. Couldn't afford to fill the tank, so gave it to my ex-wife."

"Your ex-wife?'

"Yeah, I got married in my early twenties. Peggy turned out to be a bad apple!"

"Don't talk about women that way, Sam."

"Excuse me, but it's the truth." He looked angry. Dizzy returned to the topic of cars.

"Where do we go to find a reliable used car?"

"Let's go to a car dealer and look around."

"OK. How about next Sunday morning?"

"It may be closed on Sundays."

"I just remembered. The other day I noticed that a church nearby had a sign advertising a benefit car sale. It's this coming Saturday afternoon. I'd rather give my money to a church than a car dealer."

"Give me the address, and I'll meet you there."

"No, come to think of it, Saturday afternoon is no good for me. I have a date with a nice gentleman."

Sam glanced at Dizzy, looking angry and suspicious.

"You tell me now…"

"Just kidding."

*****

The sun suddenly disappeared. Dizzy and Sam sped up because it was getting cold. While walking briskly, the elderly lady was mulling over the plans she had just made with a man she had met only a couple of days earlier. What would her children think of her buying a car at her age? What would the neighbors think if they found out that she was going on a long-distance trip with a homeless man half her age?

"I don't care," she said under her breath. "I really want to go to the desert again and see the spring flowers. They should be beautiful this year after that winter rain."

"What are you mumbling? Are you changing your mind about our plans?"

"No, it's a done deal."

She nodded her head to signify her agreement with Sam's idea. They resumed their walk, only stopping whenever they spotted beautiful flowers. Then it started raining, and Dizzy felt cold.

"I should've taken my umbrella. I left it at home after you made fun of me."

"Sorry, I didn't mean to. Have my Salvation Army jacket. It'll keep you warm."

"But you'll get cold without a jacket."

"Don't worry, you get tough when you're homeless. Besides, you're more precious than me."

She was touched by his generosity and his gentle manners, thinking her late husband would never have acted like that. *What a boor he was*, she thought to herself.

The wind was getting stronger, splashing her face with rain. She suggested going back to her house for a cup of hot tea. Sam accepted her invitation.

*****

When they reached Dizzy's house, they were astonished to see Devil standing on the front porch. He was shivering in the cold rain. She grabbed him and held him tightly in her arms.

"Devil, my baby, where have you been all this time?" His only answer was a *meow*. Sam defended him.

"Of course you can't talk, Devil. Oh well, you're back. That's the main thing. You look like you were well fed for the last few days, right, Dizzy?"

"I'm sure some people took care of him." She looked at her cat. "I wish you could talk, Devil."

"Let Devil be! Why do you want a cat to talk?"

"Because if I knew who took such good care of my dear cat, I would want to thank them."

"Never mind, at least Devil wasn't lost in the woods. Stop being so curious, Dizzy!"

"You're right, Sam. But it'll remain a big mystery."

"Maybe someday the mystery will be solved."

"I hope so!"

Sam left shortly after Dizzy made hot tea for both of them and they drank it in the kitchen, sharing her only cup. The rest of the day, she took special care of her beloved cat, spoiling him with a special dinner and his favorite treats. In the evening, she made vegetable soup for herself and went to bed early, with Devil curling up close to her.

In the night she had a strange dream. A man knocked on her door, carrying her orange cat in his arms. The elderly man didn't look like her late husband. He gave the cat to her and they started chatting. Before she knew it, the man was inviting her to dance the next weekend.

When she awoke in the morning, Dizzy wondered if her dream meant something. Could it have been a clue to the person who took care of Devil and fed him for a few days? She chased away the idea. The identity of her cat's providential caretaker would remain a mystery. But for how long?

CHAPTER 4

On Saturday morning, Dizzy jumped out of bed at eight thirty. She quickly grabbed the nearest clothes at hand and got dressed while talking to herself.

"I never heard my alarm. I'll be late for my appointment with the French lady."

She was on her way at nine o'clock and practically ran downhill. When she reached her destination six blocks away, she rang the pink house's doorbell. The seven-year-old boy opened the door and welcomed her.

"Good morning."

"Good morning. I'm late for my appointment with your mother," said Dizzy.

"That's OK, on the weekend she's always on French time." He shouted. "Mom, a funny lady is here for you."

His mother appeared at the front door in her bathrobe and chided her son. "Marc, don't speak that way. It is not polite."

"But Mom, the lady is dressed funny."

"That is no reason to be rude." She turned to Dizzy. "Good morning, come on in!"

"Your son's right. I must look funny. I was in such a hurry! Oh well…"

Dizzy looked at herself and burst out laughing. In her haste, she had put on two shoes that didn't match: a black one on the right foot and a brown one on the left foot. Also, she hadn't paid attention to color coordination, orange pants with a pink winter jacket. She addressed the French lady.

"I apologize for my funny appearance."

"Look at me, I am still in my bathrobe. You seem to be out of breath. You did not have to hurry that much. Today is Saturday. Make yourself comfortable in the living room while I prepare coffee."

"Can I help, Mom?"

"No, Marc, it is grown-up time."

"Can I watch TV?"

"No, go to your room and play with your little cars."

"But I want a croissant."

"How do you know that I bought croissants for breakfast?"

"I saw them in the kitchen last night."

"OK, go and get one, and give us privacy."

"What's privacy?"

"It means that you leave us alone."

Marc went to the kitchen and came back through the living room on the way to his bedroom, dragging his feet and carrying a croissant in one hand. His mother, after watching him, turned her attention to Dizzy who was sitting on a couch.

"What would you like in your coffee? Cream? Sugar?"

"Nothing."

"You're so easy to please! People in the neighborhood were right, you are a nice lady in spite of your…"

"Funny outfits and weird ways."

"I did not say that."

"But you thought it. It's OK. I'm used to people being critical of me. It amuses me."

She got up and both women went to the kitchen to prepare coffee and put the croissants on a plate. After they returned to the living room, Dizzy broke the ice while her hostess was pouring coffee into two mugs.

"Let's introduce ourselves. I am Dizzy Hunter."

"Is Hunter your husband's last name?"

"No, my maiden name. I always liked my last name, so I kept it when I got married."

"Your husband did not object?"

"At first he did, but I was stubborn, so I won!" She giggled. "What's your name?"

"My name is Chantal Fisher."

"May I call you by your first name, Mrs. Fisher?"

"You may certainly do so, but Chantal is difficult for Americans to say. Believe me, people here have called me all kinds of names. Sometimes Candle. Even Chanterelle once."

"Chanterelle, like the mushroom? That's so funny!" Dizzy caught herself and apologized to Mrs. Fisher for making fun of her first name.

"No apologies needed. I laughed it off myself. But since that time, I go mostly by Chris in this country. Of course Americans say that name much better than Chantal."

"For sure, but it's such a nice name! May I call you Chantal?"

"Thank you for making the effort."

"You're welcome. It's nice to have several names at different times of your life. It's like reinventing yourself." She gave an abbreviated version of her first name change. "My parents had named me Daisy. But now I go by Dizzy."

"At first, I thought it was your last name."

"Nope. My husband called me that way because he thought I was often silly. Now I like that name, because it's easy for people to remember it."

"Like my last name, Fisher. When I first met my future husband, he suggested I might keep my maiden name, as we often do in France. But I decided to take his last name. We were so much in love." She began to cry. "He's dead now. I am a widow."

"So young! Was your husband sick?"

"No, a car accident."

"I remember reading something about it in the paper a while back, but I forgot the details. What happened, if I may ask?"

"We were returning from a party at somebody's house in the mountains. Black ice on the road, you know, winter weather in Oregon. Our car plunged off a cliff. He died on the spot. Miraculously, I was not even hurt." She sighed. "A few days later, I found out that there was an opening to teach French at one of the middle schools in town. The regular teacher decided to take a maternity leave of absence for the rest of the school year, which was granted. I took a chance with no teaching experience and was hired right away."

"I bet the school was happy to find a native speaker of French."

"I was lucky to find a teaching job in December. I started teaching in early January. Believe me, it was a hectic Christmas vacation."

"I bet it was good for you emotionally to think of your new job."

"Sure, it took my mind off the death of my husband. But it was very bad for my son, poor baby. I was so busy taking care of business and preparing for the job!"

For the next five minutes, the two women drank coffee and ate croissants in total silence. Then they turned to the business at hand.

"Have you thought of my offer, Dizzy?"

"Yes, I'll do it."

"I thought of paying you one hundred dollars a week. That is for two hours every weekday."

"Two hours a day? But the elementary school is so close to your house. It's only a ten-minute walk."

"Yes, but I want you to make sure that Marc has breakfast before school and a snack in the afternoon before I come home. I would like you to come at eight o'clock every morning. Here is a key to the house."

"OK. I'll take good care of Marc."

"Thank you, Dizzy. I need to have peace of mind while on the job. You seem to have what we call in French joie de vivre. That's why I wanted to hire you."

"It's true that I have joie de vivre. Hopefully it will be contagious."

"I should warn you. My son has been especially difficult since the death of his father. Are you sure that you can handle him?"

"You can count on me. My main purpose in life is helping people, especially now that my husband is dead."

"Your husband died?"

"Yes, I'm a widow too. We have a natural bond. We both lost our husbands in 2018, the same year, with a big age difference. I'm a lot older than you. How old are you, Chantal?"

"Thirty-five."

"And I'm eighty, but who cares? Betty Friedan was right when she said, 'Aging is not "lost youth" but a new stage of opportunity and strength.' As long as I live, I want to be active for others' sake and for myself."

"I admire you! But how come I did not find out right away that your husband died last summer? We live in the same town and I read the local paper every day, including the…what do you call them in English?"

"The obituaries. Oh, I had a very short obit about him. It's what he wanted: his name, his age, and only a few words about him. It only appeared for one day, sometime in July last year."

"We were in France at that time. No wonder I didn't find out about his death. Anyway, at the time I didn't know you and your husband. But one day while taking a very long walk, I noticed the 'For sale' sign in front of your big house. Out of curiosity, I looked at the flyer, and some neighbors saw me…"

"My former neighbors?"

"Yes. They told me about you and your husband. They told me you wanted to move to a smaller house a few blocks away. We chatted about you for a few minutes. They described you as a small woman looking younger than her age and very happy. That is how I recognized you, when we met on the street the other day."

"I see." She paused. "It took several months to sell the house. I finally moved just recently to a rental house a few blocks from my former place."

"I guess that the big house felt empty after your husband's death. How old was he when he died?"

"Ninety-six."

"Do you miss him a lot?"

"Yes, sometimes."

"We will have to share more, now that we know we are both widows. But let me return to the childcare business. When I have to leave in the morning, Marc is still asleep. Sometimes you'll have to wake him up."

"I'll make sure he gets to school on time, and I'll bring him home after school in the afternoon. You can trust me."

"Good!"

"Tell me more about your son. You mentioned earlier that he has a problem, but he seems to be happy."

"Marc is hiding his problem very well."

Chantal got up and went to make sure that her son's door was closed so that he couldn't overhear the conversation in the living room. She came back and had a sip of coffee, sitting in her chair and facing Dizzy across the coffee table.

"Actually, his problem started before the death of his father, but it has become worse. He is mixed up about his identity and angry with me about his French name."

"French? I thought his name was Mark?"

"But it is spelled with a 'c' at the end, like in French."

"And he's angry about that?"

"It is a whole identity problem. You see, he is the only black kid in his school. This neighborhood is almost exclusively white. When we adopted him in Africa, we did not think that it would be a problem. He was a baby then, a few months old. Later, when he was of preschool age, we considered moving to a different neighborhood. But my husband was against it because he built our house. He was an architect, a good one."

"I'm sure."

"At age four, Marc started asking questions about his identity. He would say, 'Why am I different from all the other kids?' We never hid from him the fact that he was adopted, but he desperately wanted to be like all the other kids around here."

"I understand. I'll try to take care of his identity problem."

"How?"

"I don't know myself just now."

"I trust you. It looks to me you have a generous heart and imagination."

"I'll try my best."

"Thank you. How soon can you start?"

"I'll let you know after I make plans with my nephew for a trip to the desert."

After that discussion, Dizzy was ready to leave and do some-thing less serious. She said goodbye to Chantal and went off. Once at home, she changed her clothes and shoes to look more "normal," fed Devil, and had a light lunch followed by a short nap.

*****

When Dizzy woke up, it was time to walk to the nearby church for the car sale. Sam was already there, inspecting some of the used cars. She greeted him and someone served them coffee in mugs that had a picture of the church. Then she spotted a small green car.

"How about that one in the corner, Sam?"

"I didn't see that one." He carefully examined it. "Too expen-sive. Six hundred dollars!"

"I've got enough money."

A man overheard them and approached them, ready to negoti-ate the price on behalf of the church.

"What can I do for you? You seem to like that car. You can have it for five hundred dollars. Do you want to drive it around the block?"

"I'll let my nephew do that," Dizzy answered.

"I'll need to hold your driver's license," the man said looking at Sam.

"I don't have a driver's license just now. Let it lapse a few years ago. Was too poor to have a car."

The improvised salesman stared at him. "Then you can't drive that car. It's illegal to drive without a license." Dizzy intervened, but the man wouldn't budge. She had an idea.

"Sam, let's get that car anyway. I love the color, and it's a low price. Let's take a chance!"

"OK. If you say so, Auntie."

The man looked at them suspiciously again, but he agreed to the sale when Dizzy pulled out her checkbook. Sam immediately sat in the driver's seat, and she sat next to him in the passenger seat. They drove slowly out of the church parking lot. Suddenly in the next block, as they were gaining speed, the car lost a front tire. Sam stopped the car and they jumped out of it.

"That car was a rip-off," he said. "What do we do now, Dizzy?"

"Walk back to the church parking lot and try to get my money back."

"Let's go and talk to that guy. You tell him to give you back your check."

The churchman was busy selling another car. Sam and Dizzy had to wait five minutes before speaking to him. When they told him what had happened, he refused to give the check back to Dizzy.

"It's a benefit. You can't get back what you gave to the church."

"You're a thief!" Sam said angrily.

"Watch your language, young man! All I can do is to give you the name and address of a buddy of mine who fixes used cars."

"I don't need your car mechanic. I have my own buddy nearby. Let's go, Dizzy."

"What about calling your friend?" she suggested. "Maybe he could come help us right away."

"Good idea!"

Sam called his friend, who came right over in his truck with all the necessary tools. In no time, he had fixed the car but wouldn't accept any money for his work. He pointed to the car. "This isn't a very good car. Why did you decide to buy that one?" he inquired.

"I liked the color, and we decided to buy it," said Dizzy. "It's my fault. I was silly."

"You should take your time to buy a used car."

"But we needed a car right away."

"Why are you in such a hurry?"

"We want to go to the desert. Soon. The flowers will start blooming in February, right, nephew?"

"Something like that."

The car mechanic gave them a funny look and left. They returned to their respective seats in the green car and drove to her place.

*****

Sam and Dizzy spent the rest of the afternoon looking at desert flowers and 2019 bloom times on her computer. She got excited and wanted to make plans for the trip.

"Sam, now that we've got a car I'd like to go to the desert very soon."

"Why?"

"Because of my new job."

"A new job? At your age?"

"There's no age for what you love to do." She laughed. "Could we go around mid-February? Like over the Presidents' Day weekend?"

"That's a bad weekend for traffic, lots of people on the road. Why go so early? Because of your new job?"

Dizzy was somewhat reluctant to tell Sam about her job, fearing that he might try to talk her out of it under the pretext of her advanced age. She felt no need for this kind of protectiveness and wanted to be totally in charge of her own life. Her secret reason for wanting to go on the trip around mid-February: she wouldn't be on duty over the four-day Presidents' Day school holiday.

Suddenly an idea popped into her head. "It's my birthday that weekend, February 17. Sam, suppose your driving on the trip would be my birthday present from you."

"OK, birthday girl, that's a deal!"

"Someone told me the desert flowers might bloom early this year, because of the winter rains. We could go to the Mojave Desert and stay at low elevations where the flowers bloom first."

"Anyway, that car might not make it higher."

"What do you have against the car we got?"

"I hate green cars. Used to have a red one. Fine car!"

"We can paint it red after the trip. But green is a good color for the desert. There aren't many trees there."

"Smart remark!"

"Besides, green is a symbolic color for environmentalists, like me. Are you an environmentalist too? Are you interested in the issue of climate change?"

"Nope, I've got too many other problems."

"But, Sam, our planet is doomed if we don't do something right now."

"Don't lecture me. I have enough problems living on the street: freezing cold in winter, rain, rats, fleas, you name it…"

"And rough people."

"I can handle that. You fight back. Physically or in words. You have to talk like them."

"Do you have to use bad language?"

"Sure, you can't afford to forget the street language. If you speak too nicely, they think you're a weakling, a nobody."

"But I've never heard you use bad language when you talk with me, especially about plants."

"I'm like a chameleon. I can adapt to the people I'm with. Like with you, no reason to use bad language, except to show off."

"Will you promise to watch your language on the trip? Bad words don't shock me, but they add nothing to what you want to say."

"Yes, ma'am, promised! Makes me feel like a little boy, but you're so nice to me."

"Because I bought a car for the trip?"

"Yeah! And the food at your place. Plus, you're a very interesting lady, for your age!"

"Stop reminding me of my age! I like to think a long life is like separate chapters in a book, some better than others."

"A better chapter now?"

"Yes, definitely! My cat is back, and I've been getting acquainted with new people in the neighborhood while looking for Devil. And I met you, a new friend! I only wish I knew who took care of my cat for a few days."

"Still a big mystery, but who cares?"

"I do!"

He was getting tired of Dizzy's obsession. Why did she care so much about her cat's temporary caregivers? But she went on talking about it.

"Sam, I want to tell you about a dream I had after we found Devil on the porch last Wednesday. I dreamed of an elderly man knocking on my door with my cat in his arms. After he gave Devil to me, we chatted for a while and he ended up inviting me to a dance. Could that be the mysterious person who fed Devil for a few days?"

"I don't know. But enough of that!"

Sam was starting to feel jealous of that mysterious man in Dizzy's dream. Without saying goodbye, he abruptly left her house and started walking downhill in search of a good place to spend the night.

CHAPTER 5

On Sunday morning, Dizzy was awakened by her cat. He had left his sleeping spot next to her on the bed and was roaming through the house, meowing for breakfast. She jumped out of bed and went to the kitchen barefoot. She filled Devil's bowls with food and fresh water while talking to him.

"Poor baby, you must have been really hungry. You were complaining so loudly that it woke me up!" She looked at the clock on the stove. "My goodness, already nine thirty. Usually I feed you earlier. I was sleeping so soundly, I never heard you until a few minutes ago." She was feeling guilty. "I'm a bad mother for you. Not like the stranger who fed you so well for a few days. But who was that? Could it be the man in my dream?"

Devil seemed indifferent, paying attention only to his food and water. Dizzy got exasperated.

"Cats are supposed to be curious by nature. I'm like a cat, so curious! Devil, where were you for a few days? I wish you could talk and tell me."

Dizzy ended her monologue and went to the living room to start her morning mindfulness practice. She sat cross-legged on the floor, still in her pajamas, and focused on the sounds of the birds outside.

Thirty minutes later, she went to the bedroom and got dressed. She decided to take a walk after a quick breakfast consisting of a banana and a cup of herbal tea. Bundling up to go out in the chilly morning air made her think of the impending trip to the desert where it would be warm. She had to talk to Sam as soon as possible to firm up their plans. Maybe he was still in the neighborhood, in which case she might be able to see him. But her immediate plan was to walk to Marc's house to discuss more details with his mother about her new job.

When she reached the pink house, Dizzy noticed that there was no car in the driveway. Maybe Chantal and Marc had gone to church. Suddenly Cindy appeared on the street with her baby strapped on her back.

"Hello, Dizzy. How nice to see you on my morning walk!"

"Hello, Cindy and Daffodil."

"The other day you promised to visit us again soon, but you've been a stranger! Would you like to keep me company today? My husband is away on a job."

"But it's Sunday, you might want to go to church."

"I don't go to church just now. It's too difficult with the baby." She caught her breath. "I have coffee ready at home."

"OK, that sounds good."

They walked together to Cindy's house. Then the baby took a nap while the two women drank coffee and chatted happily.

"Dizzy, when we met for the first time you were looking for your cat. Did you find him by any chance?"

"Oh, he mysteriously appeared on my porch. A miracle. I was so happy! He looked very good. Someone must have been taking care of him." She got agitated. "I wish I knew who it was, but it's a mystery."

"The main thing is that your cat is back, isn't it?"

"But I'm so curious, I want to know who took care of him."

"Why are you so curious?"

"It's my nature. I'm like cats. Anyway, curiosity is happiness."

"What do you mean?"

"Curiosity is what pushes you to make fun new discoveries."

As Cindy looked perplexed, Dizzy went on. "I don't mean to lecture. But when I was working as a nurse, I started noticing that curious patients were happier than others."

"What about yourself?"

"I've always been curious. I've always loved the unexpected, you know, unfamiliar experiences. My parents discouraged that. They were only comfortable with familiar people and things. But my natural curiosity never really left me. When I was still a child, one of my uncles showed me his collection of skulls that proved man's evolutionary origin. I was fascinated, but I didn't tell my parents because they might have objected to those ideas." She paused, flashing back to her past. "My uncle also took me on hikes, pointing out plants to me. That made me curious about nature, and I still am."

"I wish I was curious like you, but I'm so busy being a wife and a mother."

"Do you have time to read?"

"Only when Daffodil's asleep."

"I'll lend you a book called *Curiosity*. The author believes that curiosity is a crucial dimension of a fulfilling life, and I totally agree."

"You're a smart lady!"

"I've lived longer than you have. Now that I'm retired and a widow, I have more time to read and think. I'm convinced that old people, if they aren't curious, will die earlier than they should, or at least be unhappy."

*****

The conversation came to an abrupt end when Cindy got a phone call from her husband. Dizzy discreetly left, waving goodbye to Cindy and the sleeping baby. She decided to go and see if Chantal was home to discuss a starting date for the childcare job. This time the car was in the driveway. She rang the bell and Marc's mother opened the door.

"Hello, Chantal. We need to set a date for me to begin my job."

"Hello, Dizzy. Come on in! Good timing, Marc is at the playground. He wanted me to drop him off on our way back from grocery shopping. He likes the playground on Sunday morning while people are at church."

"Why does your son like to go to the playground when it's deserted? He doesn't like people?"

"Maybe he feels different."

"I understand."

"Let's talk!"

They went to sit in the living room. Chantal couldn't wait to tell Dizzy about Marc's current behavior.

"As I told you earlier, my son is very difficult to handle these days. Are you sure you want the job?"

"Yes, I want to try to make him happy, share my joie de vivre with him."

"Great!"

"But I should let you know I'll be taking a trip for a few days in February. I can ask one of my friends to replace me in my absence."

"Where are you going?"

"To the desert, to see the flowers"

"Alone?"

"No, I have a nephew who wants to go with me. He can do all the driving. It would be in mid-February."

"Wonderful! There is a four-day school holiday around that time. I can take care of my son over the long weekend."

"That's exactly why I decided to go then."

"You are a great lady, so organized and so happy!"

Chantal felt grateful toward Dizzy but at the same time somewhat envious. By what magic would an elderly woman be able to make Marc happy when she, his mother, had mostly failed? That was a bitter mystery to her.

"I wish you good luck with my son. Can you start taking care of him as early as tomorrow morning? It's already late January, almost February, and I still have to prove myself to the school officials. I'd like to continue in the same position next year if the regular teacher decides to resign."

"Relax and focus on your job. You can trust me."

"I have confidence in you, after checking on you with your former neighbors. They told me repeatedly that you have become strange since the death of your husband but that you are totally trustworthy."

Dizzy chose not to be offended by her former neighbors' gossip. She hugged Chantal, feeling happy that she was able, in spite of her age, to help a young woman and her son through a difficult period of their lives. She was about to leave when Marc knocked on the front door. His mother rushed to let him in.

"Did you have a good time at the playground, Marc?"

"Yeah, except I saw a scary man on a bench. There was an empty whiskey bottle on the ground."

"Probably a homeless man."

"No, Mom, he was well-dressed."

Dizzy was pretty sure it was Sam, but she said nothing. She remembered that her new friend had surprised her on Saturday, coming to the church parking lot in his new Salvation Army outfit and well-groomed. After he left her house in the evening, he must have decided to stay in the neighborhood and sleep there overnight. The playground, with its benches, would have been a perfect place.

After an embarrassing moment of silence, Dizzy said goodbye to Chantal and Marc and left hurriedly. On her way back to her place, she looked for Sam; but by that time, he must have left the neighborhood.

*****

The next morning, she was at the pink house at eight o'clock. She used the key that Chantal had given her to enter the house. The seven-year-old boy was still in bed.

"Hi, Marc. Time to get up and have some breakfast."

"I'm not hungry."

"But you've got to eat before school."

"I don't want to go to school today. I've got a tummy ache."

"Too bad! But I brought you a surprise."

"For me? What is it?"

"My cat."

"Where is he?"

"In my car. I'll bring him in after you get dressed."

"OK, just a minute. Where's your car?"

"In the driveway."

"Can I see it?"

"When you're dressed."

51

Marc jumped out of bed and appeared two minutes later, dressed for school. He peered through the living room window.

"I see a green car in the driveway. Your car?"

"Yeah, I just got it."

"Neat, I like it."

"I chose a green car because my cat is orange. It's a good color combination."

"Cool! Can I bring Devil inside?"

"You know his name. How come?"

"When we saw you on the street the other day, you were calling him. He was lost. How did he come home?"

"One day I found him on my porch. He looked fine. I wonder who took care of him for a few days."

"Maybe a neighbor."

"Maybe. Anyway, it's time for breakfast, Marc. I'll bring Devil in while you eat."

The little boy went obediently to the kitchen. He prepared a bowl of cereal and milk, while Dizzy went to get her cat out of the car. When she returned, Marc was eating his breakfast. He took Devil in his arms and let him drink milk out his bowl.

"It's time to go to school, Marc. Get your jacket and boots. It's raining."

"May I take Devil to school? We start with show-and-tell every day."

"My cat isn't a puppet. He'll come home with me after I drop you off."

"Too bad! But I get a ride in your green car?"

"Good idea, it's raining really hard right now."

"If I go in your car, I don't need my boots, Mrs.…"

"You may call me Dizzy."

"That's a funny name for an old lady."

"Who cares about my age? We're going to have fun together. I've got other surprises for you."

"Tell me."

"Not now. Go and find your boots. We're walking after school this afternoon, rain or shine."

"You are a funny lady! Oops, Mom doesn't like me to say that."

"I don't mind people calling me a funny lady. Life has to be fun!"

"I like you, funny lady!"

"Time to go to school, Marc."

The two of them and Devil got into the green car. She dropped off the little boy at school. Then she drove home with her cat.

*****

In the afternoon, it was cloudy but not raining. Dizzy felt good walking down to Marc's school. On the way, she was mumbling to herself.

"Walking will be good for the boy. I took my car this morning because of Devil. But walking is healthier for people and better for the environment." She reflected for a minute. "Let's be honest, Dizzy. You wanted to try your new car on your own. But enough of that. I'm glad that Sam, oops my nephew, will be driving on the trip."

She reached the school just in time. Marc came out of the schoolyard. He was alone. He greeted her. "Hi, Dizzy."

A little boy ran past and asked, "Who's Dizzy?" Marc looked the other way and didn't answer.

"How come you didn't you answer that boy?" Dizzy asked him as they were walking home.

"It's none of his business."

"Are you ashamed of me?"

"Nope. But that boy insulted me the other day."

"Insulted you?"

"Yeah, he asked me where I come from."

"And you found that insulting?"

"Yes. He meant I look different."

"I guess you feel lonely in an all-white school?"

"Yeah, and it's even worse when my mother shows up."

"Why?"

"'Cause my mom is white. The kids here are so curious about that." He turned to Dizzy. "You're different from those kids. The first

53

time we met on the street, you didn't look surprised at all that my mom was white."

"I'm used to biracial families. At my church…"

"What's biracial?"

"That's like your family. Some people are white, some are black. Who cares? It's like having a green car and an orange cat. It's fun to mix colors. It makes you joyful."

"You're a happy lady. Not like my mom, she's so sad since my dad died!"

They walked in silence for a while. The sun appeared, brightening the plants in the neighborhood gardens. Dizzy wanted to pull Marc out his somber mood. She noticed some yellow plants and started quizzing the little boy.

"Do you know the name of those bright yellow flowers?"

"Yes, it's winter jasmine."

"Very good! And that shrub with yellow flowers?"

"It's winter sweet."

"How come you know so much about plants?"

"My dad loved nature and he taught me a lot. We used to go on walks together. He was an architect. He built our house."

"I know, your mom told me."

"I like our house, but I wish it was yellow."

"Your mom might like the house the way it is, pink."

"I know why she likes pink. It's the color of her sister's house in France."

"Your aunt? Do you like her?"

"Yeah, a lot. She adopted an African boy, like me. My cousin is even darker than me."

"What's his name?"

"Nicolas. He's ten years older than me. But we get along fine."

"How often do you see him?"

"Every time we go to France. We stay with them." He paused. "I wish my mom would take me to France this year. I could see my cousin Nicolas. But she'll have to work this summer."

"You liked it better when your mom was staying home?"

"Yes and no. She's very strict. Not like my dad. It's not her fault, she was brought up that way."

"Her family in France is conservative?"

"What's conservative?"

"Being afraid of change. Sticking to what you're used to."

"I get it! That's why my mom called me Marc, with a 'c' at the end. It was her father's name."

"I guess you'd prefer Mark, with a 'k' at the end?"

"Yeah, I'd feel more American."

Dizzy was starting to understand the little boy's identity problem. She felt for him. Would she be able to make him happier? How? Suddenly, lighting struck. Marc seemed to enjoy colors. She would do something about it right away.

After getting back to Marc's house, Dizzy called her hairdresser. Could he give her an immediate appointment? By chance, he was free in the late afternoon. After Marc's mother came home from work, Dizzy rushed to the closest bus stop and reached her hairdresser's salon just in time. She had him color her hair bright green.

*****

On Tuesday, Marc was up and eating breakfast in the kitchen when Dizzy arrived. He heard the front door open and didn't recognize her at first.

"Good morning, Marc. What's the matter? Did I surprise you?"

"You look different."

"Just my hair. I thought I'd color it green for a change."

"To match your car?"

"If you want to put that way. But I thought you'd like it anyway."

"I like it, but..."

"But what?"

"You look funny."

Dizzy burst out laughing. She told Marc she had wanted to be a clown but that her parents had objected. So she said she went to college and majored in nursing instead. All through her story, she was making funny faces, and Marc laughed so hard that his cereal and milk was pouring down his face. They looked at each other, unable to stop laughing.

"You look funny too, Marc. But it's time to walk to school. Go and wash your face, quick."

"I know. I'll make faces like that when I feel miserable at school."

That afternoon when Chantal came home from work, she found Dizzy and Marc practicing funny faces. She was glad she had found a good caretaker for her son.

*****

But the next day turned out to be quite different. On the way back from school, Marc wanted to show Dizzy "his" playground. After using the slide and the monkey bars, he sat down on a bench next to his caretaker. He pointed to another bench across the play area.

"Look, that's where the scary man was sitting last Sunday."

"Why do you say the man was scary?"

"'Cause he was smoking pot."

"So what?"

"Only bad people smoke pot."

"Your mom told you that?"

"Yes."

"She's wrong to say that. Lots of good people do, now that it's legal in Oregon."

Marc became angry and defensive. Dizzy felt bad and wanted to distract the little boy.

"Look, I see something shiny on the ground by that bench. It might be dangerous. You've got better eyes than I do. Go and pick it up."

Marc complied and came back carrying a small pocketknife. "It must belong to that scary man," he said.

Dizzy recognized it as Sam's knife.

"It's my nephew's! I'll give it back to him next time I see him."

"So the scary man is your nephew? Why did he sleep on the bench?"

"He's just homeless right now."

Marc was confused. He didn't want Dizzy to be associated with a scary man that was homeless. He needed to feel totally secure with his caretaker. He wasn't ready to confront anything unfamiliar.

Dizzy was turning the situation over in her head, wanting desperately to find a solution to the turmoil she had partly caused for Marc. She said cheerfully. "I have an idea. What if I bring my cat tomorrow morning and we take him to your school? I could ask your teacher to let you use him for show-and-tell, and I would take Devil home afterward."

"Cool!"

The next morning, they put the plan into action. Everything went very well at school. Marc was elated and finally gained his classmates' respect, thanks to an orange cat called Devil. And Dizzy was happy: her joie vivre had proved to be contagious!

CHAPTER 6

Dizzy liked her childcare job very much. She enjoyed sharing her enthusiasm for life with Marc. After the successful show-and-tell with Devil, the little boy had been feeling less alienated from his classmates. In fact, he seemed to have forgotten his identity problem for the time being.

On their walks to and from school, he and Dizzy would look for early-blooming flowers in front yards. Together they had invented a game: the first one to spot some crocuses could make a wish that would hopefully be granted. After a mild winter, crocuses began blooming early in 2019. Marc was the first one to spot some in a yard close to his school.

"I won, Dizzy! My wish is that you bring Devil for another show-and-tell. This time was so much fun! I'm sure the kids in my class want to see your cat again."

"I'm glad to hear that! Wish granted! Can you ask the teacher what day would be good?"

"You do it."

"OK, but it will have to be after my trip…"

"A trip? Where are you going? When?" Marc asked with fear in his voice.

"To a desert in California to see the flowers. Just for a short while, at the time of Presidents' Day weekend. I'll leave on a Thursday and return the next Monday in the evening. It's a three-day weekend, no school for you on that Monday, and your mom won't go to work either. She didn't tell you about it?"

"Nope."

"I told her that a friend of mine can take care of you on Thursday, when I'll be absent before the school holiday."

"I can walk to school by myself on that day."

"I bet your mom won't let you."

"I know. She thinks I'm a baby."

That afternoon Dizzy talked to Marc's teacher after school. They set a date in late February for another show-and-tell with Devil. Then she and Marc slowly walked home, discovering more crocuses of various colors on their way. The little boy shouted with joy whenever he spotted some, but he sometimes turned pensive. Dizzy was sure that he was apprehensive about her trip, and she felt bad about it.

*****

After Chantal returned from work in the afternoon, Dizzy went home and she soon had a phone call from her son.

"Hello."

"Hello, Mom. This is Julian."

"You haven't called me for a long time."

"I've been really busy. Can you babysit Ruby this evening? We'd lined a babysitter, but she called an hour ago to say that she changed her mind. I take it you're free."

"Yes, I can take care of Ruby tonight." She giggled. "But now that Ruby is six, you shouldn't talk about babysitting."

"OK, Mom. Denise and I are going out for dinner. Can I pick you up at six o'clock?"

"I can drive down myself."

"You have a car? I thought you sold the family car."

"I did, but I got a new one."

"Mom, you promised to give up driving."

She chuckled. "But I realized that my driver's license is good for two more years, so I've got to use it."

"You can't drive in the dark."

"You're right, because of my vision. So I'll accept your offer of a ride."

"Is six o'clock OK?" Julian asked impatiently.

"That's fine. See you tonight!"

Dizzy knew better than to prolong the conversation with her son. She wanted, in vain, to reassure him that the car she had bought was a used one and very cheap. Some of her children and their spouses were afraid she wouldn't leave any inheritance for them.

She started thinking of her brood: in addition to her youngest son Julian, she had one son in Chicago and one daughter in Dallas, both married and with kids ready to go to college. They were too busy to call her more than a few times a year. Only Julian, her local son called more often, especially when he and his wife needed child-care for their daughter.

For a moment, Dizzy reflected on her younger years. In her early twenties, she had married Albert who had turned out to be a domineering man and a miser. After she gave birth one year apart to a boy and a girl, her husband had declared that two children were enough mouths to feed. Ten years later, she wanted a third baby and had to pretend that it was an "accident." Albert let her choose a name for their third child, after having imposed his choices for the first two: Henry (his father's name) and Jennifer (his mother's name). Dizzy had decided to call the baby Joy if it was a girl and Julian if it was a boy.

Her youngest son had always been nice to her, but his wife was a selfish and uppity woman who treated him like a little boy.

*****

Julian arrived at six o'clock in a bright, new car. He was dressed in a dark suit and wore a tie. He noticed his mother's amused glance and apologized. "Mom, I know you prefer casual clothing, but Denise told me to get dressed up tonight. It's a business dinner."

"Whatever your wife says, you must obey…"

"Mom, don't start that, please."

"OK, I won't say any more." Speaking deliberately in a cheerful tone, she asked, "Did you see my new car, I mean my used car, in the driveway?"

"Yes, and frankly I don't like it."

"Why?"

"The color is sickening. Like your hair."

Dizzy laughed. "Oh, I forgot. I had my hair colored green to match the car. Too bad they didn't have an orange car to match my cat's color. Of course, they had white, and black, and plain gray, but..."

"I hate to pressure you, Mom, but Denise will be mad if we're late."

"OK, coming." Dizzy moved to the front door. "Let's not get princess Denise angry," she said sarcastically.

"Don't be so mean!"

"You're right, but I can't help thinking it's funny you've become a slave to your wife."

"Funny? You find it funny?"

"You might as well laugh about things you can't change."

Out they went to his car, and twenty minutes later, they were in Julian's driveway. Six-year-old Ruby, still in the dark blue uniform of her private school, rushed out of the house. She opened the car door for her grandmother and hugged her affectionately. The little girl's mother came out dressed in an elegant black winter coat and a bright red scarf. She hardly paid attention to Dizzy and went straight to the car where Julian was waiting. Denise waved goodbye to her daughter and mother-in-law, and the couple left for their formal dinner.

Ruby led the way into the house. She went straight to the kitchen and put some chocolate chip cookies on a plate. "Let's have a good time, Grandma. Chocolate chip cookies are a good appetizer."

"But they're for dessert.'"

"*Shh*, don't tell my mom we had them before dinner. Let's go sit in the living room. I have to tell you a big secret."

"A big secret?"

"Yeah, promise not to tell Mom, she'd be mad."

"I promise."

They sat down on the couch, close to each other. Dizzy liked her granddaughter's vibrant personality. She was like her dad when Julian was growing up, but his wife had changed him. Denise was an authoritarian woman who took life too seriously and had dragged Julian into her business ambitions. She never laughed and had no sense of humor whatsoever. No wonder Ruby adored her grand-mother who laughed so easily!

"Tell me your secret, Ruby."

"I want to change my name."

"Why?"

"Someone called me Jade the other day."

"Funny!"

"It's not funny, Grandma. Don't laugh at me."

"Sorry, but it reminded me of the time when I was called Pansy instead of Daisy."

"Your name was Daisy?"

"That's the name my parents gave me, but I changed it." She laughed. "Lucky you! Someone might have called you Turquoise."

"Or Turkey." The little girl started laughing. "You're right, it's funny." Then she became serious. "Please, Grandma, help me choose a new name. And keep it secret for now."

"Why?"

"'Cause my mom chose the name Ruby for me. She likes jew-elry. Not like you."

"I enjoy simple life more and more. Don't tell your parents, but I got rid of so much stuff after your grandpa died. He was a pack rat. I'm the opposite."

"What's a pack rat?"

"Someone who wants to keep everything." She laughed. "I'm very happy with as few things as possible and my cat."

"Why did you call him Devil?"

"Because orange cats are supposed to be especially playful." Dizzy didn't tell her granddaughter that Devil was her own name for a few years. She had an idea. "Let's choose your secret name. How about Joy, since you've got joie de vivre?"

"What's joie de vivre?"

"It's a French expression that Americans use. It means that you're happy with your life."

"Like me and you!"

Ruby forgot about her secret name for the time being. She decided it was dinnertime, went to the kitchen, and returned with cold chicken on a plate and a bowl of salad that her mother had prepared. She put the food and two plates on the dining room table, which was covered with a nice lace tablecloth. Then she opened a drawer containing silverware.

"No silverware for me, Ruby. Food tastes better when you eat with your fingers," Dizzy said cheerfully.

"I love you, Grandma. My mom is too fussy. You remember the time you took me to the playground when I was four?"

"Yes, and you were so dirty when we came home! Your mom never asked me to take you to the playground again."

Dizzy and Ruby laughed as they ate chicken and the dressed salad with their fingers. But the grandmother caught herself being too judgmental of Denise and felt that she was turning Ruby against her mother. She purposely changed the topic.

"I bought a car the other day. Guess the color."

"White."

"To match my hair? Wrong!" She paused. "Look, my hair is green. I got it colored the other day to match my car…"

"I noticed it, but I didn't say anything. Grandma, you're a funny lady."

"That's that Marc told me."

"Who's Marc?"

"A seven-year-old boy that I'm taking care of. I walk him to school in the morning and back home in the afternoon."

"He needs you for that? I'm only six and I walk to school all by myself."

"It's different. Marc lost his dad not long ago and has lots of problems."

"What problems?"

"I can't go into it. You'd not understand. But I try to help him as much as I can."

"How?"

"Marc loves my cat, so I take Devil to visit him, and sometimes to his school for show-and-tell."

"Could you do that for me? Please, Grandma!"

"I'll think about it. For now, let's play a game before your bed-time. You choose the game."

Ruby went to her room and returned with a large box that said Ladders and Slides, a pretty simple board game based on chance. Dizzy didn't like it very much but complied. She noticed her grand-daughter took it very seriously.

"Ruby, I mean Joy, why do you like this game?"

"It's fun to throw the dice and to play with you."

The elderly lady took note of the fact that the young child val-ued companionship, an essential element of joie de vivre.

"Grandma, I wish you'd come more often. We have fun together."

"I'd come more often if I felt welcome here, but..."

"I know, my mom doesn't like you. And you don't like her either."

"How do you know that?"

"I heard my dad and mom talk last night. They thought I was asleep, but I was just pretending."

"What were they saying about me?" Dizzy couldn't help asking.

"That you're very strange. Dad told Mom about your green car. They think it's crazy to spend money that way. Dad called his brother and sister about that, and they agreed."

The grandmother regretted involving a child in her twisted family affairs. In order to put an end to this second-hand report, she declared that it was bedtime for her granddaughter. After the little girl got into her pajamas, Dizzy tucked her in and read her a happy story. Pretty soon the child went to sleep.

*****

An hour later, Julian and Denise came home. They were visibly drunk, she even more than her husband. Dizzy interrupted her read-ing and looked at them without a word of disapproval. Denise went to the kitchen to get a glass of water.

"I see two dirty dinner plates in the sink, but no forks and knives. What happened?"

"Ruby and I decided we didn't need silverware."

"You ate with your fingers? Disgusting!"

She returned to the living room with a glass of water in one hand. Being unsteady on her feet, she tripped over a nice Persian carpet and fell on her face. The glass broke into small pieces on the floor.

"Help me, Julian."

Her husband came to the rescue and helped her stand up. While gathering the pieces of broken glass from the floor, Julian apologized to his mother. "We had to drink a lot. I told you it was a business dinner." He paused. "But I'll be fine driving you home. It's close and there's very little traffic tonight."

"Let me call a cab."

"No, Mom, I swear I'll be fine." He turned to his wife. "Denise, I'm taking Mom home now."

"OK, Julian, be careful!"

Dizzy gathered her things and off they went, Julian leading the way. Once behind the wheel, he seemed to sober up. When they reached her neighborhood, he became somewhat emotional and nostalgic.

"I'd like to see the playground where I had such a good time when I was a child. You used to take me there. Do you mind the small detour, Mom?"

"Not at all. You should come more often to see your old neighborhood and me!"

"You know, my job and family keep me busy."

"Especially your selfish and domineering wife," Dizzy muttered under her breath so that Julian couldn't hear.

They had reached the playground and he had parked on an adjacent street. Still sitting in the car, he was contemplating the moon shining over the trees, seemingly happy and relaxed. Suddenly he jumped.

"There's a man sleeping on a bench."

"So what? It's his right. The playground's a public place…"

"But Mom, if it's invaded by homeless people, the value of houses around here will go down."

"Stop thinking of money all the time!"

"I can't help it, I'm a realtor. Fortunately, you sold the family house nearby before this invasion. By the way, what did you do with the money?"

"You're talking about the money from the sale of our house? I invested it at the bank."

"You mean, the inheritance to be shared between the three of us?"

"Yes."

"Denise says that both Henry and Jennifer have all the money they need. She could use my share of the inheritance to start her own business, a jewelry store. By the way, did you know that you can give more money to one of your children?"

"You mean, give you a bigger share of inheritance?"

"Yes."

"Well, I'm not ready to give it all away. I dip into the bank account when I need something, like a car."

"What do you need a car for?"

"For trips, like I want to go to California to see the desert flowers."

"By yourself? You can't drive that far. I forbid you, Mom."

"Don't act like your father! Now that he's dead, I'm free to do as I please." She continued in a calm but resolute tone of voice. "In fact, I've lined up a driver for the trip to the desert."

"Who is he? Probably someone who wants to rip you off."

"You're wrong. He's…" She stopped in her tracks. She usually answered the driver was her nephew, but Julian would know she was lying.

Suddenly the man on the bench turned over, and she immediately recognized Sam. He stood up and greeted her.

"Hi, Dizzy. What are you doing here in a car with a man at this hour of the night?"

"He's my son."

"That's what you say!"

"Julian, tell him you're my son."

"Who is he, Mom?"

"A new friend."

"A man who sleeps on a bench in a playground?"

"What's wrong with that? Besides, he's my driver."

"You're crazy. Denise was right…"

"Leave me alone!"

Dizzy stepped out of Julian's car and he sped away. She stood there, shivering in the cold winter night. Sam got up from his bench and covered her with his sleeping bag. He offered her a small pipe. She didn't know what it was but took it. He patiently taught her how to smoke pot. After first hating it and coughing, she slowly started enjoying it and relaxed.

A while later, Sam suggested taking her home. They walked briskly uphill side by side. When they reached Dizzy's house, she reminded him of the trip, asking him to come at seven o'clock on the day of departure. He silently grabbed his sleeping bag from her shoulders and headed back downhill to the playground for the rest of the night.

Dizzy entered the house and went to bed right away, feeling lonely. In the night, she had nightmares about her children.

*****

A few days went by. Dizzy was preparing for the upcoming trip. She first made sure that there was enough food in the house for Devil. This time she had hired a semiprofessional pet caretaker recommended by her veterinarian. Who cared about the expense? That was a good use of her money. She wouldn't have to worry about Devil running away, like the last time she went on a trip.

The week of the trip came fast. It was mid-February already. On Monday, Dizzy went to take care of Marc as usual. When she entered the house, he was still in bed. She tried to tease him. "Lazy boy!"

"I don't want to go to school today."

"Why not?"

"'Cause you're leaving. The holiday weekend is coming up. My mom told me last night."

"But I'm not leaving till Thursday, and I'll be back next week."

"That's too many days without having fun with you."

"Let's have fun today! We could play again the crocus game on the way to school."

"Can I have another wish granted?"

"If you're the first one to spot crocuses today, yes!"

She had challenged the little boy, and it worked. He got out of bed, dressed quickly, and gulped down his cereal breakfast in the kitchen. He was the first one out the front door. On the way to school, Dizzy pretended not to see any crocuses. Marc screamed with joy when he first spotted some close to his home.

"I won again," he said triumphantly.

"Bravo! We didn't notice those the other day."

*****

Marc's mother returned home late that afternoon. She found her son and his caregiver playing cards.

"Mom, I won again!"

"You won the card game?"

"No, I was the first one to spot crocuses this morning. Now I can have another wish granted."

"What is your wish?"

"I dunno. Anyway, it's between Dizzy and me."

Chantal kept quiet. She was becoming more and more envious of the elderly lady who knew how to make Marc happy. She retired to her bedroom under the pretext of a headache. Actually, she wanted to cry in solitude.

A few minutes later when Dizzy got ready to leave, Marc cheerfully said goodbye to her with a mischievous look, and he hugged her for the first time.

The next two days he was calm and didn't fuss about going to school. He looked like he had something up his sleeve, but he was keeping it a secret for the time being.

CHAPTER 7

On Thursday, Sam arrived at Dizzy's house at seven o'clock in the morning and rang the bell.

"Are you ready?" he asked while she opened the door. She was in her bathrobe, holding Devil in her arms. He came in, dressed in khaki pants and a gray t-shirt under his Salvation Army jacket.

"Can you take Devil? He's hungry. I should feed him and get dressed."

Sam took the cat in his arms and spoke gently to him while petting him. "Devil, aren't you going to miss Mama? Who will feed you while she's gone?"

"Not Maggie for sure," said Dizzy while filling the cat's bowls with food and water, "I hired someone more dependable. She was recommended to me. I told her to be especially careful not to leave the front door open." She paused. "I still don't know who took care of Devil after he ran away last time…"

"Who cares?" Sam shrugged his shoulders.

"I'm curious, I want to solve the mystery."

"We'd better leave soon, we've got a long way to go," he said impatiently. He released Devil who rushed to his bowl of food.

"OK, I'll be ready in a minute. Here's the key to the red car, excuse me, the green car," Dizzy said jokingly.

Sam went out. He grabbed his backpack and an old blanket from the front steps and put them in the trunk. He was behind the wheel, ready to go, when Dizzy came out of the house, dressed in black ski pants with a green sweater under her pink winter jacket. She was carrying a small gray suitcase that she threw on the back seat and sat down in the passenger seat, and off they went into the cold winter morning.

"You forgot to lock the front door," said Sam with tongue in cheek, "Devil might escape."

"Stop teasing me, Sam! But that's a good joke," Dizzy said with a burst of laughter.

"OK, I'll behave." He continued while looking at her. "It's so exciting to go to the desert with you!"

"Wouldn't you rather go with someone your own age?"

"Age isn't that important. You're so much fun!"

"I try my best." She became pensive. "Yesterday I called my brother in northern California and my sister in Palm Springs again. They both insisted they have room for both of us, in separate places."

"I'd feel more comfortable sleeping on a bench in a park."

"Are you afraid they'll think you're a gigolo?"

"I don't care what they might think. But my privacy…"

"Your privacy? What do you mean?" She started giggling. "You think you have privacy on a public bench?"

"Usually people leave you alone, except for the cops and your son."

"That little devil!"

"By the way, what are your brother and sister like?"

"Didn't I tell you? My twin brother lives in a commune called Crazy Bear close to Willits in Mendocino County. I think he's become a minimalist like me."

"And your sister?"

"The opposite, she's the ultimate consumerist. She's rich. At twenty, she married an older man that was wealthy. Trophy wife, I guess. When he died she inherited a lot of money, she remarried a while back, but I haven't met her second husband yet. All I know is that they live in a gated retirement community in Palm Springs."

Sam remained silent. He had secretly decided he'd like Dizzy's brother, but certainly not her sister.

*****

After a while, their conversation resumed, but it took a different turn. They were planning the road trip. They would stay overnight in the commune in northern California and reach southern California the next day. The final destination was the Desert Wash, a "life zone" in the Mojave National Preserve where wildflowers should already be blooming. According to an article they had read online, 2019 was expected to be a spectacularly good year for desert wildflowers due to the winter rains.

At lunchtime, Dizzy and Sam stopped in a rest area on Interstate 5 and ate the healthy sandwiches she had prepared. They also took turns drinking lukewarm tea out of a thermos she had brought along. In the afternoon, after a stop at a gas station to fill up the tank, Dizzy napped or meditated most of the time while Sam was driving. One of them occasionally drew the other's attention to the scenery, but mostly they remained silent.

Just before dinnertime, they reached the small town of Willits in west Mendocino County on Highway 101. Sam noticed a sign giving directions to a garage sale. He pointed it out to Dizzy and asked if she wanted to go. At first she declined. "What for?" she asked.

"Just to see what they've got." He giggled. "All kinds of junk, I'm sure."

"OK, you've made me curious. Let's go!"

They went to the place indicated on the sign, parked the car across the street from the garage sale, and walked over to look at the junk. A few minutes later, they were about to leave when Sam discovered a banjo. He grabbed it and started playing a beautiful tune. The young woman in charge asked if he was a musician. He answered angrily. "Yes, sometimes. Had to sell my guitar. Now all I've got left is a harmonica."

"You can have this banjo for a good price. I've also got a ukulele. It's hiding over there. It's a good one," she said, hoping to make a sale.

Sam found the ukulele in the middle of some junk items and inspected it. "Looks like it's in good shape. Too bad, I haven't got any money." He laid down the banjo and ukulele.

"I can give you a good price for both," said the young woman, desperate to unload some of her merchandise at the end of a cold day, during which very few shoppers must have shown up.

Dizzy cheerfully intervened. "I've always wanted a ukulele since I had to quit playing the piano because of my arthritis. The ukulele should be easier on my hands." She thought for a minute. "I'll get the ukulele for myself and the banjo for my driver, if you give me a good price."

After bargaining with the young woman, Dizzy wrote a check and handed it to her. Meanwhile Sam, whistling happily, had gone across the street and put the two musical instruments into the car trunk. He asked for directions to the Crazy Bear commune where Dizzy's brother lived. They got into the car and took off. By then it was pitch dark.

They had to ask for directions several times. The commune was in a remote western part of the county, high in the mountains. When they finally found it, they parked the car in a soggy place in front of a makeshift building with a few lights on. A tall man wearing only dirty jeans and a loud tie-dye t-shirt came out and hugged Dizzy, as soon as she got out of the car.

"Hi, Sis. Good to see you. It's been quite a while."

"Hi, Adam."

"My name is Sunbeam now."

"Excuse me, how could I forget?" She giggled. "You told me on the phone."

"No problem. And this must be Sam, your new lover…"

"Cut it out, Sunbeam. Sam is my driver, not my lover."

"Just kidding!" He turned to Sam who had also gotten out of the car and gave him a warm bear hug. "Hi, buddy! You're just in time for dinner. Let's go to the dining room."

Dizzy and Sam followed Sunbeam into the communal building. Dinner was ready. Someone had put steaming food platters on a long wooden table with no tablecloth. Grownups and kids came out of the kitchen with piles of chipped plates, mismatched old forks, and pitchers of tap water. They sat down on benches around the collective table, greeted the guests, and then grabbed plates and forks and helped themselves to the food. They started eating the food and drinking the water while talking and laughing. The noise was deafening, but Dizzy liked the joyful atmosphere in spite of her tiredness.

She was sitting between Sunbeam and Sam, enjoying the simple vegetarian food, along with plain tap water in semi-clean glasses.

After dinner, Sunbeam showed his guests the sleeping quarters and asked them to choose a place for the night. There were family cabins, couples' cabins, a longhouse for men, and a separate women's compound. Dizzy chose the women's place and said that she was ready for bed after a long day of traveling. Sam brought her small suitcase from the car to her sleeping quarters. After they set a time for departure the next morning, he left without saying a word. Sunbeam waited patiently to give his sister a good-night kiss. When he turned around, he didn't see Sam. He called him twice but got no answer. Since it was starting to rain, he hurried to the longhouse.

In fact, Sam had heard him, but he wanted privacy in the car to drink whiskey from a bottle he was hiding in his backpack. After he drank half the bottle and smoked pot in his pipe, he went to sleep.

*****

In the early morning, Sam awoke at the sound of someone trying to open the car door. It was a bear. He decided that music would be the best way to calm the animal and pulled his harmonica from his backpack. The bear went away, disappointed that he would get no food. Sam kept playing, composing a song about his encounter with the bear. Suddenly Sunbeam appeared out the dark.

"What are you doing, Sam? It's five o'clock and really cold. I was awake all night, thinking that you had left."

"And leaving your sis stranded? Not like me, she's too nice."

"You slept in the car? Aren't you cold? Come to the longhouse."

"No, thanks. How about you, buddy, up so early?"

"Got a job to do. Every morning I'm in charge of chasing the resident bear away, before the school bus comes for the kids."

"The resident bear? The one that woke me up this morning?"

"He came to your car? He wanted food. In winter, there's not much food for bears around here. We have one bear that roams around here every day in search of scraps of food. He seems to feel at home here. On nice days, he sits in his usual spot, basking in the sun and quietly watching the kids play around him. That's why we call him Crazy Bear, and we named our commune that way." He paused. "He must have been the one coming to your car this morning. You got scared, buddy?"

"Nope. I used to go camping. Once a small bear was licking my face in the night. I guess he was after my suntan lotion."

"Cool! But do you know where Crazy Bear is now?"

"No, he left when I started playing my harmonica."

"You're a musician?"

"Yeah, sometimes."

"Awesome! We can play together. I've got my guitar in the longhouse."

"Go and get it right now!"

Sunbeam walked away in the darkness and soon returned with an old guitar in hand. Meanwhile, Sam had gotten his new second-hand banjo out the car trunk. They improvised together for a couple of hours while smoking pot.

Suddenly Dizzy appeared, dressed warmly and in winter boots. She approached the car, carefully avoiding the wet patches on the ground.

"I heard you from the women's place." She turned to Sam. "Did you spend the night in the car? It must have been very cold." She noticed the half-empty bottle of whiskey on the passenger seat and immediately understood why Sam wanted privacy and wasn't too cold during the night. She decided to take it in stride and cheerfully asked the two musicians to play more songs.

"No, it's time for breakfast," said Sunbeam.

Sam grabbed his leather jacket and put on his sneakers. He followed Dizzy and her brother to the dining room. After morning greetings, they sat down and joined the grownups and kids eating porridge. A few minutes later the school bus arrived and parked in front of the communal building. Attentive adults made sure that the kids had finished their breakfast and kissed them goodbye. After the kids boarded the bus, carrying colorful school bags, Sam and Dizzy decided it was time for them to leave too. They said goodbye to commune members and hugged Sunbeam, who asked them to drop by on their way back from Southern California. They both promised to do so and quickly walked to the car in the pouring rain.

"Sam, I see a half-empty bottle of whiskey on my seat. Did you get drunk last night?"

"You're right. It was so cold!"

"Don't give that kind of excuse. I wish you were like my brother. He's sober now." She paused. "After his divorce…"

"From his wife Eve?"

"Yes. How do you know her name?"

"He composed a sad song about her. When he sang it to me this morning, he was crying like a baby." His voice became emotional. "Why did they get divorced?"

"She got tired of jokes about Adam and Eve," Dizzy said, laughing.

She caught herself when Sam looked at her, seeming surprised by her flippant answer.

"I shouldn't joke about serious things." She hesitated. "I hate to tell you, but they got divorced because of his drinking."

"Like me. I didn't tell you earlier, but my wife left me for the same reason."

Dizzy didn't say anything, but she was secretly plotting to do something to help him stop his excessive drinking.

*****

They drove slowly in the mountainous area of Mendocino County. Afterward, they remained silent for a few hours. They stopped for lunch at a rest area south of San Francisco. It was sunny and getting warmer, so they sat at a picnic table and ate the rest of the sandwiches Dizzy had brought from home. Sam offered her a ukulele lesson. She accepted readily and went to the car to get her new instrument. He patiently showed her how to strum the ukulele.

After they took off again, she kept practicing in the car while Sam drove and gave her musical advice. She enjoyed his teaching. But when the traffic became heavier, he concentrated on his driving, and she took a nap.

They reached the Palm Springs area late in the evening. It was nine o'clock at night when Dizzy called her sister and apologized for being so late. Esther told her to come for a snack before bedtime.

"My husband's out anyway. I have to be up for him when he comes home."

She gave her sister directions to their gated community and the code to enter the complex. Dizzy conveyed the information to Sam who kept driving in silence. When they got to Esther's house, there were formal greetings, but no hugs. The guests were invited to sit on a leather couch by a huge glass coffee table in the living room. Their elegant hostess, still a beauty at age seventy, was dressed in a pale green conservative outfit and had an impeccable hairdo. She proceeded to treat them to an abundant assortment of cheese and crackers surrounded by bunches of grapes on a large wooden board. She also served wine in crystal glasses.

Dizzy was really tired but tried very hard to stay awake and make light conversation with her sister, while Sam kept quiet most of the time. He was visibly becoming more and more uncomfortable in this stifling atmosphere. After a while, he thanked Esther for the snack and wished a good night to Dizzy, who was falling asleep on the couch. Before their hostess could say anything, he left under the pretext of wanting to explore the town before going to bed.

He went to the car and drove out of the complex. In fact, he had decided to park the car in some back alley and sleep there overnight, after drinking the remainder of his bottle of whiskey and smoking some pot.

Around midnight, Dizzy woke up to the sound of arguing in the entrance hall. The lights were on. She glanced up and saw a tall man with blue eyes and sparse gray hair. He looked like he might be around seventy. He was wearing black pants and a Hawaiian shirt, facing Esther who was speaking loudly in an angry tone of voice.

"It's so late! You promised to return earlier this time, Oscar. My sister and her driver arrived hours ago."

"I'm sorry, but I was winning big at the blackjack table tonight, and it was hard to leave the casino," he said sheepishly.

"You could have gone tomorrow instead," she said, getting really angry.

"Tomorrow, Friday evening, on a four-day weekend? No thanks, it's going to be really crowded…"

"You're right. But you could have skipped the casino this week."

"Are you kidding?"

"Gambling matters more to you than I do. Let's face it, you're an addict…"

"Don't call me that way. It's not true!"

The argument stopped abruptly when Esther noticed that Dizzy was awake. Immediately reverting to her role as a submissive socialite, she made introductions in a sweet tone of voice. "Oscar, this is my sister. Dizzy, this is Oscar, my husband."

"Glad to meet you, Oscar," Dizzy said in a sleepy voice. "Let me introduce you to my driver Sam…"

"He left a few hours ago," Esther said, lowering her voice.

"What? Where did he go? He didn't tell me."

"You had fallen asleep on the couch. He told me he wanted to explore the town." She shrugged her shoulders. "Who knows where he went. Men are like that…"

"Stop it, Esther!" Oscar shouted while approaching her with a threatening look on his face.

"We'd better go to bed. It's past midnight," said his wife in a soft voice. "Dizzy, let me show you your bedroom."

"Where's my suitcase?"

"Probably in the car with your driver. I can give you toiletries and a night gown."

"Thank you, Esther. But I'm concerned about Sam."

"Don't worry, I'll hear the car when he returns." With a sneer in her voice, she continued. "I sleep lightly. Oscar is snoring loudly sometimes."

Dizzy followed Esther to the guest bedroom without a word. Her usual joie de vivre had totally disappeared: she was concerned about Sam and felt for her sister who had gone from a tyrant (her first husband) to a passive-aggressive individual (her second husband). Oscar was obviously a meek individual dominated by his wife, but he had demonstrated that he could have unexpected fits of violent anger. For her part, Esther was making a pretense of being a submissive wife. Dizzy saw it as a hopeless game between the two of them.

The guestroom suite consisted of a spacious bedroom and a large bathroom. Across the hall was a smaller guestroom with its own bathroom. Dizzy hated the size of the rooms and the whole house. She sighed, imagining Sam under a bridge, playing his harmonica and drinking whiskey. Was he happy that way?

She caught herself thinking of her new friend too much. She came back to reality when Esther brought her a nightgown and toiletries. "Is there anything else you need, Dizzy? By the way, I wish you'd change your name…"

"It's the name that Albert chose for me. My husband was a macho, like your first husband, but at least he had fun ideas, once in a while. As you know, he used to call me Dizzy Daisy, and it became Dizzy after a while. I like that name. It makes me laugh."

"Laughing isn't my style these days."

"Stop being so negative, Esther! Life is too short, it's to be enjoyed."

"I know, but there isn't much for me to look forward to."

"Come on, there are so many pleasures in life!"

"Like what?"

"Like petting a cat or looking at flowers…"

"Do you still have a cat?"

"Yes, a new one. His name is Devil, and I love him. But lately I've been more and more interested in plants."

"How come?"

"I met a homeless man that knows a lot about plants. He took botany classes in college…"

"A homeless man? Watch your money!"

"Why are you so suspicious? Anyway, money is meant to be used. Like, I sold our family house and bought that car, just to go to the desert to see flowers in bloom."

"And you hired a driver?"

"Sam?"

"Be careful, he looks like a drifter."

"How can you say that? You don't even know him. He's a friend…"

"A friend? Really? Look at what he did tonight. He went away, and he's not back yet and it's past midnight." She continued in a serious tone of voice. "What will you do if he left for good with your car?"

"Sam would never do that."

"We'll see."

Esther wished her sister a good night and left. Dizzy brushed her teeth, got undressed, and put on her sister's elegant, black lace nightgown. She went to bed and managed to sleep fairly well in spite of her concern for Sam. She had sweet dreams about flowers in the desert.

CHAPTER 8

The next morning at eight o'clock, Esther knocked gently on Dizzy's door.

"Are you awake? Breakfast will be ready in ten minutes. Oscar is cooking today. Sometimes he wants to take over the kitchen, and he makes a mess." She entered the bedroom. "I hate it when he hangs around the house. Fortunately, he goes golfing every day for hours." She handed her sister a bathrobe. "Enough of that. You'd better hurry."

"Is Sam here?"

"No, I'm afraid he left for good."

Dizzy did not panic. As a positive thinker, she was confident that Sam would reappear sooner or later. She did not want to share Esther's negativism and pessimism. Besides, she was sure the would-be botanist wanted to see flowers in the desert and act as her teacher.

She put on the red silk bathrobe her sister had handed her, brushed her hair, and washed her face with cold water. On her way to the dining room, she overheard a conversation between the spouses in the kitchen.

"How many eggs, honey?" Oscar asked.

"Six, two for each. I doubt that Sam will be back."

"If he does, I can cook some eggs for him later."

"He might come for the food. He's probably a free loader. My sister told me horrible stories about him."

"Really? Tell me!" Oscar said, sounding both curious and alarmed.

"I'd better not tell you now. Dizzy will be here any minute for breakfast. I'll tell you later. But I hope Sam doesn't come back at all. He's a drifter. He might steal…"

"You're so suspicious!"

Dizzy joined them in the kitchen and pretended not to have heard their conversation. Oscar, dressed in a blue silk bathrobe, was cracking eggs and cooking them in a big frying pan. She started helping to prepare the toast. The hostess was hovering over them, as if she feared female competition. When she set the table in the dining room, she placed Oscar and Dizzy far apart from each other. The two of them still managed to have a conversation under Esther's watchful eye.

"Do you know how I met your sister, Dizzy?" Oscar asked.

"No, she didn't tell me."

"At a golf club dance. Esther doesn't play golf unfortunately, but anyone can come to the dances." He turned to his wife. "You were so beautiful that night in your little red dress! I thought you were sixty, and you danced really well." He drank some coffee and continued his story. "We started dating shortly after the dance. On our fourth date, I made a confession to Esther about my age. I was sixty-five then. To my surprise, she told me she was the same age. I felt right away I could propose to her. She accepted, and we got married a few months later."

"You were happy to move into my big house. You were renting such a small place at the time!" Esther said.

"And you were happy to catch a divorced man so soon after your husband died! I bet you hated being single," Oscar snapped back. He turned to Dizzy. "How about you? I heard you also lost your husband recently. Are you thinking of getting remarried?"

"No."

"A pretty woman like you shouldn't be alone. If I was still single…"

"Oscar, that's enough," Esther said angrily.

"Stop playing helicopter and hovering over me!" said Oscar.

Dizzy hated to see him having another fit of passive-aggressiveness. Fortunately, at that very moment, the doorbell rang, and Esther went to see who it was. Sam appeared, looking disheveled. "Welcome, Sam, you're just in time for breakfast," the hostess said in a sweet voice. "Dizzy wasn't sure that you would come back and get her," she added dramatically.

"Of course I'm back. We want to go to the desert."

"It's going to be crowded today, you know, the first day of a long weekend," Oscar said timidly.

"Are you trying to keep us here?" Dizzy burst out laughing. After receiving no response to her joke from either of her hosts, she addressed Sam who was still standing by the front door and asked if he had eaten breakfast. He answered, intentionally stressing every word to shock the snobs who were listening to him.

"Yeah, in a fancy place downtown. I couldn't find a cheap joint anywhere. The manager handed me the menu, and when he took a look at me, he said 'Free for you, but make it quick.' He directed me to a booth in the corner, and I ate as fast as I could, and plenty. No charge, cheap breakfast!"

Dizzy applauded. "Good for you, Sam! Anyway, there must be plenty of rich customers around here."

"But that's no reason to beg like that," her sister said with a scornful expression on her face.

"He didn't beg, Esther. It was offered to him," Oscar stressed in a conciliatory tone of voice.

"That's one interpretation." She pursed her lips and turned to Sam. "And where did you sleep?"

"That's a long story."

Dizzy thought it was smart of him to be evasive about his night. She remembered that there had been half a bottle of whiskey left in the car. She figured he must have drunk it and fallen asleep afterward. A confrontation between her sister and Sam would be pointless. Diversion was necessary.

"I should get ready to leave. It will be quick, since my suitcase is already in the car." She giggled. "I'll wear the same clothes as yesterday and change into my light clothes on the way." She turned to Esther. "Thanks for letting me use your nightgown and bathrobe. Should I leave them on the bed?"

"You can wear them tonight, and keep them later if you want."

"Thanks, but they're not my style. Oops, I goofed again! Seriously, I don't need such beautiful things. I'm not trying to attract a man."

She heard Esther say sotto voce, "That's what she says. But she's got that gigolo." Dizzy pretended not to have heard and went to the guest bedroom, while Oscar began clearing the breakfast table.

*****

Ten minutes later, Dizzy said goodbye to her hosts and promised to return with her driver in time for dinner. When she got to the car that was parked in the driveway, she saw Sam already behind the wheel. She sat down in the passenger seat, and they took off. They stopped at a nearby gas station to fill the tank.

"I couldn't wait to get out of your sister's house," Sam said once they were on the highway leading to the Mojave Desert.

"Why?"

"Those people made me sick. Your sister henpecks her husband, the guy is too dumb to fight back."

"That's their business. It's obvious that my sister has become a domineering woman and Oscar is a passive-aggressive. They make a good pair, they deserve each other. I take it with humor, it's like soap opera. In a way, it makes me laugh."

"Dizzy, I thought you were a nice lady…"

"But when there's nothing I can do for someone, I give up. I treat it like comedy, and that makes me patient with the people." She reflected for a minute. "Speaking of theater, I'm about to change into my light clothes."

"In the car?"

"Why not? There aren't many people on the road right now."

Dizzy proceeded to change her clothing while Sam was driving. Suddenly a police car appeared behind them and pulled them over. A young policeman came around on the passenger side. Dizzy lowered the window while continuing to undress.

"Ma'am, what are you doing?"

"Just changing clothes."

"A driver called us to report that an elderly woman was disrobing on the highway. Is that you? Show me your papers."

She handed him her driver's license. He inspected the card. "I see you're eighty years old. You shouldn't disrobe in public, especially at your age."

"What's wrong with that?" she asked.

"She can do what she wants in our car," Sam said angrily. The policeman took a good look at him. "Don't play smart with me." He reflected for a minute. "You look like a young fellow, what are you doing with that shameless elderly lady?"

"That's none of your business," Dizzy intervened. Then she patiently said, "He's my nephew. He's driving me to the Mojave Desert to see the flowers."

"Sure! He looks more like a drug dealer. The border isn't far. Show me your papers, young man."

"I don't have a driver's license."

"You don't have a license and you drive?"

"Yeah, things happened so fast. Dizzy got a used car and…"

"I'm getting suspicious of you two. Come with me to the police station!"

Sam followed the order. Once they arrived at the police station back in Palm Springs, Dizzy decided to call her sister. Oscar answered the phone. After he heard her story, he said that he had a golfing friend who was a captain at that police station. He called his friend and an hour later, the problem had been solved. Sam had to promise to get a driver's license when he got home, and Dizzy got a lecture about decency in public places. But for now, they were free to go.

They discussed the situation on the way to Mojave National Preserve. Sam turned to Dizzy while driving.

"That cop was arrogant and full of himself."

"But he was right about your driver's license. I told you to get one before the trip."

"I don't want to deal with those idiots at the DMV."

"You can't be a rebel all the time. You've got to conform a little bit."

"I know. But don't lecture me!"

"At least that incident showed me that Oscar has some power. I thought the guy had no say, but he sure got us out of trouble quickly. Every situation has good sides."

"You're an eternal positive thinker, cool lady!"

"You mean 'shameless elderly lady.' Wasn't that funny when the cop called me that way? It reminded me of an incident, I mean an accident, when I was three."

"A funny story?"

"Yeah, and pretty disgusting. Actually, it was my first act of rebellion. I didn't know at the time, but now I'm proud of it."

"You make me curious."

"Here's my story. I already was going to preschool at age three. One day right after recess, I needed to use the restroom. I raised my hand and the teacher said I should have gone to the restroom at recess. So I stood up and went to the aisle between the desks, squatted, and peed on the floor through my underwear."

"Shocking! Of course, I'm kidding. That's a really good story."

Sam and Dizzy were laughing so much for a few minutes that they had tears in their eyes. After a while, they calmed down and saw a sign indicating that the Mojave National Preserve wasn't far.

*****

When they got to the desert, it was already noon, due to the police incident. They parked the car, the green color making a welcome contrast with the color of the sand. It was hot. Fortunately, they had thought to stop on the way and buy water. They weren't hungry, but they drank some lukewarm water out of a plastic bottle.

The flowers in the Desert Wash were sparse but spectacular: there were yellow sunflowers and sun cups, white dune primroses, and hot pink or purple sand verbena. They invented a game: the first one to notice a flower and say the name would get an imaginary brownie point. Sam won; he had twice as many points as Dizzy after an hour.

She was a good loser but got tired of the game. She started tracing a huge clock in the sand with a stick she had picked up. Together they drew a different flower at every hour around her clock. They tried to reproduce the exact size and shape of each flower and would write its name underneath. It was a fun way to learn botany and gave Dizzy ideas for teaching kids.

As it got a little cooler, they went on a walk to look for more plants. They got lost a couple of times when they left the path to admire some flowers with dazzling colors, but they found the way again. It was sheer pleasure for both of them to be in nature, even though there weren't many flowers along the path. Dizzy felt her joie de vivre returning. She started singing just as a middle-aged man suddenly caught up with them along the path.

"You must be happy," he said to Dizzy.

"You're right, I am. How about you?"

"I'm unhappy because I lost my wife in a car accident a year ago."

"So you're a widower?"

"Yeah, and it's bad. Apart from hiking in the desert, I don't go anywhere."

"You should go out and have some fun. Get a life!" Sam said.

"It's easy for you to say. At least you've got a partner…"

"She's not my partner, just a friend."

"I'm a widow," Dizzy interjected.

"You sure sound like a merry widow."

"What's wrong with that?"

"What's wrong with that? It's indecent to have fun when your spouse is gone."

"You must be some sort of preacher. Leave us alone!" Sam said angrily.

The man pulled out a handgun from his backpack and brandished it, pretending to aim at the couple. Dizzy jumped into Sam's arms.

"I'm scared," she said.

"Don't, I'll protect you." He held her tight in his arms while addressing the man. "Put that gun away, and fast!"

"I was just pretending. It isn't even loaded."

"But you scared my aunt for sure."

"Don't tell me lies! She's not your aunt. She's your lover, the way you're holding her in your arms."

Sam shrugged his shoulders and let go of her. They resumed their walk after the man went away with his unloaded gun in hand. But the pleasure was gone.

"I'm tired, too many emotions today," Dizzy said ten minutes later. She sat down on the side of the path.

"Anyway, it'll get dark pretty soon," warned Sam. "I'm disappointed, there's very little to see on this path. I told you, it's kind of early. Better come here in March or April, lots of flowers will be in bloom then."

"Like desert lilies?"

"I'm sure."

"Good! You're right, it will be better in the spring. Let's make another trip to the desert then. We've got a car now."

"A green one!"

"Let's call it Greenie."

Dizzy's mood had turned positive again. She felt like joking and being creative. On the other hand, Sam seemed to be absorbed in his own thoughts. He tried to imagine taking another long trip with his elderly friend, without getting too close to her.

"When would that be?"

"Around spring break, because of my job. Are you game?"

"Who knows? I live one day at a time. But it's tempting, on one condition, that you don't tell your sister and her husband. I don't want to see them again. They are bad people."

"I feel the same way." She reflected for a minute. "I have an idea. Let's not even go there tonight. I'll call them and make a white lie. Help me invent a story."

"You could tell them about my ninety-year-old uncle in Bakersfield and that he got sick." He reflected for a moment. "Anyway, we miscalculated. We should be heading home tonight..."

"Tonight?"

"In fact, Friday night in Bakersfield would be good. It's on the way home. Plus, my uncle gets together with his relatives every

Friday evening, and they have dinner late in some Basque restaurant. It'd be fun to join them."

"How far is Bakersfield?"

"About three hours from here."

"Let's go. I'll call Esther on my iPhone while we walk back to the car. And you can call your uncle on my phone before we take off for Bakersfield."

"Sorry, my uncle is like me, he doesn't have a phone. But he'll be happy to see us."

"Are you sure?"

"Positive!"

*****

When Dizzy tried to call her sister, Oscar answered the phone. She thanked him again for getting them out of trouble in the morning. Then she proceeded to tell him about their invented emergency: Sam had just found out that his elderly uncle was seriously ill in Bakersfield. They should stop by and visit him in the hospital. She apologized for "defecting." Oscar was very understanding and at the end of the conversation he told Dizzy how much he liked her vibrant personality. She didn't know what to make of it.

She and Sam reached the car and took off. Greenie behaved very well on the road. Sam was driving over the speed limit, but there were no cops in sight early on a Friday evening. They stopped for gas along the way and bought some more water. They finally arrived in Bakersfield shortly after seven thirty.

"Let's see if Uncle Raoul is home."

Dizzy was getting nervous. "How will you introduce me, Sam? Your aunt? But they'd know it's a lie."

"No problem, they aren't prudes." He realized his blunder and corrected himself. "They won't even ask who you are. They don't care."

He stopped the car in front of a modest house in downtown Bakersfield. His uncle wasn't home.

"He must already be in the usual place, a traditional Basque place. Let's go there. You're in for a surprise," Sam said.

Indeed, it was a surprise for Dizzy when they got to the restaurant. People were sitting on benches at long collective tables, eating Basque food. They made room near Sam's uncle for the late arrivals and asked no questions. It was a joyous and carefree atmosphere.

After dinner, Uncle Raoul asked Dizzy to dance with him. It was sheer bliss for her to be guided on the dance floor by a ninety-year-old man who was a very good dancer. She felt exuberant again.

At the end of the evening, Sam and Dizzy were offered accommodations (two separate rooms!) for the night in some Basque relatives' home. They accepted and slept very well, after a few hours of eating or drinking and dancing in good company.

CHAPTER 9

The next morning, Dizzy and Sam were invited to have breakfast in their hosts' large kitchen. Three generations of people were seated on wooden benches around a plain table. It was a simple breakfast, but everyone seemed happy to break bread with one another in a convivial atmosphere.

As a surprise, one of Sam's relatives had gone to pick up Uncle Raoul and bring him to breakfast. The elderly man made his entrance with panache. He stood erect in his white shirt and black pants with a beret on his head and a red handkerchief in his shirt pocket, the image of health and happiness. He gave bear hugs to every man in the room and kissed each of the women and children. Then he sat down next to Dizzy and kissed her on the lips.

"Sweetie, didn't you have fun last night, dancing with me?" he said to her with bravado.

"Hold it, Uncle Raoul, she's my…" Sam started to say across the table.

"Your what? Are you jealous because she and I were dancing like TV stars? It was heavenly!"

Dizzy was embarrassed by Uncle Raoul's attention. Yes, she enjoyed dancing with him, such a fine dancer! But Sam was getting visibly upset. She deliberately announced their plans for the day.

"We have a long drive ahead of us. Plus, we should stop and visit my brother again in Northern California. I should call him right now."

"Where does he live?" Uncle Raoul asked.

"In Mendocino County."

"That's several hours from here. You'd better leave soon, if you want to get to your brother's by evening. But promise me you'll be back," Uncle Raoul said to Dizzy.

"This trip was too short. Maybe we'll plan to return to the Mojave Desert another time soon. If we do, we could visit you on the way down…"

"And dance more together."

"Uncle Raoul, you'll be over ninety by then," Sam said, frowning.

"A young ninety something! Anyway, I plan to be dancing till I die. No age is too old for having fun."

Dizzy agreed but did not say so, for fear Sam would take offense. She excused herself and went outside to call her brother.

"Hi, Sunbeam. We were disappointed in the desert. It was too early, and there were only a few kinds of flowers. We're heading home, so maybe we can drop by to see you this evening."

Sunbeam sounded pleased with her idea. He insisted on having them stay overnight at the commune. Dizzy accepted his invitation and got off the phone. She returned to her hosts' kitchen, thinking of the place called Crazy Bear. She liked this name. It made her feel like dancing.

*****

Ten minutes later, Sam got up and indicated it was time for them to leave. They said goodbye to everyone, promising to come back soon. Uncle Raoul tried to flirt with Dizzy again, holding her tightly in his arms, but she got away under the pretext of having to take care of her luggage. When she got to their car, which was parked across the street, Sam was already at the wheel, fuming.

"Dizzy, you flirted with my uncle."

"He was the one chasing me."

"But you enjoyed it."

"Life has to be enjoyed."

"With an old man?"

"You know, age is less important than personality."

"But Uncle Raoul is a real woman chaser."

"Who cares? It sure was fun to dance with him last night. I liked every minute of it." She reflected for a moment. "One needs to make time for fun things. My late husband was too serious, he worked all

91

the time. He thought dancing was a waste of time. Too bad, he didn't have much fun in life."

"And you?"

"I managed to have a good time at work."

"You told me you worked in a hospital."

"Yes, for thirty-five years. After, I tried to get into art history and my husband blew it for me."

"You were mad at him?"

"No, I learned to live with it. Nursing wasn't so bad, after all. Except the schedule."

"The graveyard shift?"

"That one wasn't so bad. The afternoon and early evening shift was the hardest for me, with the kids."

"Did your husband help when you were at work?"

"He promised to do so, but he made spaghetti for dinner every time I wasn't home. The kids got tired of it and they started competing at throwing the spaghetti onto the walls."

Dizzy laughed heartily, recalling the fancy decorations on her kitchen walls. "My kids learned the custom from Italian friends. Some Italians throw spaghetti onto the kitchen wall to see if it's cooked properly. If it sticks, it needs to cook longer."

"Did your husband get mad at the kids?"

"For sure. He used to be very strict with them. He would punish them for such small things!"

"And you?"

"Most of the time I laughed at their antics. Kids are so imaginative and have so much fun! It's like some of my patients at the hospital."

"Really?"

"Yes. I remember a ninety-five-year-old woman who had been diagnosed with lung cancer and was close to death. She kept saying, 'I wonder with what sauce the doctors are going to prepare me. Hollandaise? Marinera? Teriyaki?' She made other patients laugh and forget their miseries. On her death bed, her last words were 'Thank you, chef, you did a good job. The sauce was delicious.'" Dizzy became serious. "That's the way to go. Without humor, nothing is worthwhile."

She grabbed her ukulele that was on the back seat and started practicing. Sam was listening to her, reflecting on her wisdom.

*****

It was pitch dark when they finally reached the Crazy Bear commune. Everybody was in bed, except Sunbeam who had stayed up to welcome his guests. He was reading a book by candlelight in the communal building. When he heard the car, he turned on the lights and greeted the late visitors.

"Howdy," he said while hugging them. "Did you have dinner?"

"Nope," Sam said. "I'm tired, I just want to go to bed."

He went outside, and Dizzy was afraid he might sleep in the car, like last time. She quickly came up with a good suggestion.

"Let's have a pantry raid and eat by candlelight," she said cheerfully. "Sunbeam, is there anything in the fridge?"

"There must be some leftover black beans."

Sunbeam and Dizzy brought the food and tap water to a table in the dining room and went back to get forks and glasses from the kitchen. After they turned off the lights and lit the candle again, Dizzy called to Sam, who was in the car. "Come and eat. It's going to be fun by candlelight." He came in, dragging his feet, and inspected the meager dinner on the table.

"No whiskey," he said in a pitiful voice.

"No, not here," Sunbeam said firmly.

"I'll go downtown and get some."

"Don't. I'm sure the stores will be closed in Willits. It's really late."

Sunbeam became solicitous. "Come on, dude, have some food with us." Sam complied, but after dinner, Sunbeam had to twist his arm to get him to spend the night in the men's longhouse. The two of them took Dizzy to the women's quarters, where she found a spare bed in a corner, using the flashlight her brother had lent her. She went to sleep right away.

When she woke up in the morning, it was very quiet. She found out later that the kids were gone on a two-day excursion. Many of the adults were also absent, visiting relatives or friends in other parts of the country during the long Presidents' Day weekend.

Dizzy, Sam, and Sunbeam all arrived at the dining room at the same time. They served themselves cold cereal and sat down at one of the tables. Dizzy happened to sit next to a young man who invited her to attend the yoga class he was about to teach. She accepted, and Sam and Sunbeam decided to join her. The class was held in the dining room next to a window from which Dizzy could see the resident bear roaming around.

After the class, Sunbeam wanted to keep his guests a little longer. "Why don't you stay one more day? You could do more yoga. Plus, Sam and I still have some things to discuss…"

"No, Sunbeam, not today. We've got to start going home very soon," Sam said firmly.

"He's right," Dizzy chimed in. "I promised the cat sitter to be back for Devil's dinner time. And tomorrow morning I resume my job."

"Your job? You've got a job again? At our age?"

Her twin brother sounded critical. Maybe he meant well, but Dizzy did not appreciate his overprotectiveness. She made a point to describe her job in enthusiastic terms. While doing so, she realized how strong an attachment she had developed to Marc.

Just then, the commune bus returned with the kids from their two-day excursion. They noisily ran to their parents. They were full of joie de vivre. In the meantime, Sam was getting impatient to hit the road. He and Dizzy went to gather their things from their respective sleeping quarters. They said goodbye to Sunbeam and other commune members, got into their car, and took off.

*****

After driving slowly through Mendocino County and stopping for gas, Sam sped up on Interstate 5. He looked tense and kept silent when they had sandwiches and coffee in a rest area somewhere in

Northern California. Once across the state line, he finally started to relax.

"Feels really good to be back in Oregon."

"Why do you say that? Weren't you happy at my brother's commune?"

"Yes, but no whiskey."

"I told you, my brother's marriage broke up because of his drinking problem. He seems to have totally changed his ways."

"I got the whole story last night after you went to bed. Now he doesn't touch the stuff." He fidgeted for a few minutes and burst out. "Dizzy, I want to tell you something serious."

"Tell me."

"By now I'm really fed up with risking the can. I lied to you when we first met. I didn't get that bottle of whiskey from a man I used to see at the bar. I stole it from a store. That friend of mine only gives me pot, not whiskey."

"I figured you stole the whiskey, and I forgive you. But you'd better stop drinking so much. It's so bad for your heath!"

"Why do you care about me?"

"Because I like you. Such good company! We have fun together. You're a free spirit, like me."

Sam became pensive and kept quiet for a while. Then he spilled out his thoughts.

"It's not really my fault if I've got problems. My dad was so strict! He only believed in punishment and used to beat me with a baseball bat or a rope. It's too bad I didn't grow up in a commune. Those kids at Crazy Bear look very happy. They're free!"

"Freedom is the most important thing in life, for sure. But happiness is a different thing. You've got to work at it."

"You told me you weren't happy with your husband."

"I wasn't happy with him. But I enjoyed the kids and my job. Work can be a saving grace. That's why one should never stop. Work or hobbies. Like your uncle in Bakersfield, for him it's dancing. He'll never stop. That's why he's happy."

Dizzy noticed that Sam wasn't saying anything. She didn't want to lose the chance to share her appetite for life with him. "Your hobby is music. You should play more often. There's no age for that. My twin brother took up the guitar after his divorce, at age sixty."

"You're right! Sunbeam told me that playing the guitar makes him really happy."

"You see…"

"By the way, he offered to help me."

"How?"

"He said I could come and live at Crazy Bear for a while. We could play music together. No alcohol around, there is no temptation for recovering alcoholics!" He reflected for a moment. "That might be a pretty good solution for me. Last night Sunbeam asked me to stay put. But I said to him I couldn't, I'm your driver."

"I could have gone home on the Greyhound bus."

"On the Greyhound bus? A lady like you?"

"Are you telling me I'm too old for that?"

"Not too old, but the winos…"

"Winos aren't dangerous. They can't run as fast as me."

They both burst out laughing. It was so funny to picture an old lady chased by winos that couldn't keep up with her.

*****

They remained mostly silent for the rest of the trip, watching the scenery, which was becoming more and more majestic: large Douglas firs, oak trees, and snow in the mountains. Dizzy fell into a reverie, reminiscing about the good and bad parts of the trip. She was also thinking of Devil. Hopefully nothing bad had happened to him this time. She flashed back to his disappearance a while ago. Who had taken such good care of her dear cat? She was still curious to discover the Good Samaritan's identity.

It was really late when Sam parked the car into Dizzy's driveway. However, they had a long conversation. She thanked him for driving and apologized for the unfortunate timing of the trip. "It was a bad idea of mine to go just now. You were right. Too early for many of the flowers and too rushed. I was silly!" She started singing *My name is Dizzy, Dizzy, Dizzy.* She felt joyful again as she sang.

"How come you're so cheerful?" Sam said.

"It's a waste of time to cry over spilled milk. When you fail, you've got to try again. Oh well, there will be another chance to go to the desert, I'm sure. A longer trip, maybe in late March or early April. I could take a vacation around spring break. Are you game, Sam?"

"I might not be around. I've decided to take Sunbeam's advice and move to Crazy Bear for a few months. He'll help me get over my drinking problem."

Dizzy was amazed at Sam's unexpected decision. She kept quiet for a while. Then she thought of practicalities.

"How will you get there?"

"On the Greyhound bus, with the winos." They started laughing again and then calmed down. "Seriously, could you lend me some money for the bus ticket?"

"I've got a better solution. Why don't you take Greenie along? I don't really need a car."

"Cool! That way I can drive to bars and make some money playing my banjo."

"Also, I'm sure that Sunbeam will lend you his guitar."

"Or we could play together."

After having overcome her surprise, Dizzy felt elated that Sam seemed to be ready to change his ways. She said goodbye to him in the driveway, without asking him to come in and have a bite to eat. She was so impatient to be alone with Devil and pet him again! Anyway, after returning the car key to her and getting his belongings out of the car, Sam left hurriedly with his backpack and old blanket on his back.

Dizzy took her suitcase out of the car and opened the front door. Devil rushed to greet her, and she picked him up, holding him tightly in her arms. He looked fine and was enjoying her caresses. When her cell phone rang, she put Devil down and answered the call. A French accented voice came on. It was Chantal.

"Hello, Dizzy. You are back from your trip."

"Hello, Chantal. How is Marc?"

"That's why I am calling you. You must be tired, but I cannot wait to tell you. Marc has been impossible the whole weekend. Be ready to have problems with him tomorrow morning. He told me he does not want to go to school any longer."

"I'll handle him." She yawned. "Excuse me, I just came back. I've got to feed my cat and eat dinner."

"Good night, and thank you."

"Good night, Chantal. I'll see you tomorrow."

As Devil jumped onto a counter in the kitchen, the phone rang again. It was Cindy.

"Hello, Dizzy."

"Hello, Cindy. What's up?"

"I tried to call you two days ago, but you didn't answer your phone. I thought you had gone somewhere and I didn't want to leave a voicemail."

"My apologies, I was traveling and visiting people the whole weekend. I had my phone on the silent ringer most of the time. What can I do for you?"

"My husband and I wanted to go to a movie. I thought I'd take you up on your offer to babysit. The movie is still playing tomorrow. Can you come and babysit?"

Dizzy felt pressured, being tired after the long trip. On the other hand, it was so nice to come back to many new friends! She pictured Daffodil sleeping in her crib and couldn't resist seeing her again soon.

"OK, I'll come tomorrow night. What time?"

"Around six thirty. That way Daffodil will still be up and you can feed her. We need to leave at six forty-five and we'll be back before ten."

"See you tomorrow, Cindy."

"Thank you. See you tomorrow evening."

Dizzy put her phone on the silent ringer. No more phone calls tonight! She was conflicted. An inner voice was telling her you have to take care of number one. Another inner voice was reminding her of the value of human relationships. She decided to make light of her tiredness. No regrets about her promise to babysit the next day. It was so important to help other people and share her joyfulness with them!

She fed Devil and had some dinner, sitting on the lone chair in the kitchen. Then she went to the living room and played some CDs of Satie music, *Gymnopédies* and *Gnossiennes*. She was too tired to dance, but she imagined dancing with Uncle Raoul. His joie de vivre was contagious. She went to bed thinking of him and fell asleep quickly, with Devil in her arms.

CHAPTER 10

After her long and restful night, Dizzy woke up full of energy. She felt ready to cope with Marc and was looking forward to seeing Daffodil again in the evening. She heard her cat meowing and pacing back and forth in the kitchen, clamoring for his breakfast. She fed him and had a bright idea. "Devil, do you want to come with me to see Marc? I can drive there since I still have Greenie. It would be a wonderful surprise for Marc." The cat meowed in response.

Dizzy got dressed and had breakfast. She put Devil in his traveling box and placed it in the green car parked in the driveway. She got into the driver's seat and took off, thinking of Sam.

When she entered Marc's house with her cat in the box, the little boy was still in bed, pretending to be asleep. She let Devil out, and he went straight to Marc's room, jumping onto his bed.

"Devil, you came to see me. Cool!" He sat up and gently petted the cat. "Hi, Dizzy, you're back. But it's not the day for show-and-tell with Devil."

"I know, but I thought I'd surprise you while I still have Greenie…"

"Who is Greenie?"

"Oh, on the trip we named my car Greenie."

"'Cause of the color?"

"Of course! It was so nice to have a green car in the desert!"

"I missed you, Dizzy. That lady last Thursday wasn't funny like you. And my mom cried all weekend."

"I'm sorry to hear that. But we'll have a good time today." She paused for a while. "Come on, Marc, it's time to have breakfast and get ready for school."

The little boy complied, with Devil in tow. A few minutes later, they put the cat into his box and drove to school. On the way, Marc made a request. "Dizzy, please bring Devil again this afternoon." She promised, feeling happy that her trick had worked.

The rest of the morning, she practiced strumming on her ukulele at home. She was grateful for the lesson Sam had given her a few days ago in California. She planned to play a song for Daffodil in the evening.

In the afternoon, Dizzy drove back to Marc's school with her cat in the box and parked on the street by the school. The little boy ran excitedly to her car and asked her if he could hold Devil in his arms. She said yes, thinking it would be good for both of them. She knew kids and pets have a special kind of relationship.

When they arrived at Marc's house, Dizzy was surprised to see Chantal's car in the driveway. The front door was wide open. She rushed inside, followed by the little boy who was holding Devil tightly in his arms.

"Is anybody home?" Dizzy hollered.

"Yes, I am at home," Chantal said in a plaintive voice.

"But it's early for you to be home."

"Yes, I know, I was not feeling well." She absentmindedly kissed her son on the forehead. "Marc, please go to your room. You can have your snack later. I need privacy to talk to Dizzy in the living room."

"Can I give some water to Devil in the kitchen?" Marc asked.

"Do whatever you want. I do not care."

At that point, Dizzy realized that Chantal must be distraught: she wasn't her usual overly directive self with her son. The two women sat on the couch in the living room, and Chantal started spilling out her thoughts.

"I was really depressed over the weekend."

"Marc told me. Any special reason?"

"Yes." She sighed and continued with tears streaming down her face. "Just a year ago over Presidents' Day weekend, we went on a skiing trip, all three of us. My husband and I were so happy to see Marc forget his problems for a few days!" She started sobbing. "Now my husband is gone, and I did not have the energy to take my son on a trip this year. He was *insupportable* the whole weekend…"

"You mean he was impossible," Dizzy corrected.

"Yes. What shall we do with him?"

"I've got an idea. Marc seems to adore my cat. Could he keep Devil for a few days? Is he capable of taking care of a pet?"

"I can help him." Chantal stopped crying. "What a good idea! But you will miss your cat."

"Never mind, I like to share. If it makes Marc happy and you, I'll feel gratified."

"You are such a nice lady!"

"Stop saying that, but promise me to cheer up. It's not good for Marc to have a depressed mom."

"I will try my best, with your help."

They discussed practical details about the cat's food habits and general well-being. Marc had eavesdropped from the kitchen and came out beaming.

"I get to keep Devil for a while, goodie! Can I keep him for a whole week, Dizzy? That way you won't have to bring him from home for the show-and-tell next week."

"What's the date?"

"Next Wednesday," Marc quickly answered.

"My son is so smart! He remembered the show-and-tell date!" Chantal said proudly.

Dizzy had forgotten the late-February event. She mumbled to herself. "I'll need Greenie on that day. I'll have to ask Sam to go later to stay with Sunbeam at Crazy Bear." She declined Chantal's offer to have a cup of tea, wanting to have more practice on her ukulele for the evening babysitting. She said goodbye to Marc and his mother and took off, leaving Devil in the little boy's care.

When she got home, the place seemed empty without her cat. Luckily her phone rang, pulling her out of her sense of abandonment. It was Cindy confirming their date for that evening. Dizzy confessed she could no longer drive in the dark and didn't want to walk home late at night, although their house was very close to hers.

Cindy suggested that her husband Ryan would give her a ride both ways.

*****

Shortly after six o'clock, Ryan arrived. He was a charming young man, dressed casually for the occasion. He and Dizzy chatted on the way, mostly about his computer troubleshooting business, which he seemed to love. She got lost in the technical details several times but enjoyed the chance to hear about a trade unfamiliar to her. She was so curious and eager to learn new things, especially from experts!

Once they arrived at his place, it was time for the couple to leave for the movie. Cindy, who wore a dark blue coat and black high-heeled boots, showed Dizzy the baby's food in the fridge. "This is for Daffodil, and for you I've prepared a simple dinner."

"Oh, you shouldn't have bothered," Dizzy said.

"Do you think I'd let you starve? That wouldn't be very nice."

Cindy gave a good-night kiss to Daffodil who was in her high chair, ready to be fed. Ryan also kissed his daughter affectionately, and the couple left for the movie theater.

The six-month-old baby started crying, not being used to her mother leaving. Dizzy grabbed her ukulele that she had brought along. She started playing *Row, row, row your boat*, strumming vigorously and moving her body to the rhythm. Pretty soon Daffodil imitated her and stopped crying. They were having fun!

After a while, the baby started crying again, and this time Dizzy figured she was hungry. She went to get Daffodil's food out of the fridge and patiently fed her. Afterward, she cleaned up the mess on the high chair and around it.

Daffodil yawned. She was obviously ready for bed. Dizzy took her to the bedroom, undressed her, changed her diaper, put on her pajamas, and carefully laid her in the crib. The baby went to sleep right away. Her babysitter tiptoed out of the room and went to the kitchen, thinking her main job was over.

Just as she was about to sit down and have some food, Daffodil awoke crying. Dizzy went to see what was happening. She took the baby in her arms and calmed her down by singing Mozart's lullaby in a gentle voice.

> Sleep, little one, go to sleep.
> So peaceful the birds and the sheep
> Quiet the meadow and trees
> Even the buzz of the bees.
> The silvery moonbeams so bright
> Down through the window give lights.
> O'er you the moonbeams will creep.
> Sleep, little one, go to sleep.
> Good night, good night!

Halfway through the song, Daffodil fell asleep again. Dizzy put her back in the crib. She stayed watching her for a few minutes, feeling utter bliss. Babies look so happy and peaceful when they are sleeping, their sense of bliss is contagious!

Dizzy started reflecting on her life. She wished she had worked less and had more time for fun. Now that she was retired, why was she running around constantly? She promised herself to slow down and enjoy her last few years. Maybe it would help to attend regular yoga classes and meditation sessions. But she knew the main thing for her was sharing her love of life with others.

When the young couple returned, Cindy inquired about Daffodil and went to the bedroom to check on her. Meanwhile her husband insisted on paying their babysitter. Dizzy refused, saying that friendship was much more important than money.

She put on her scarf and winter coat, picked her ukulele, and then said goodbye to Cindy. Ryan was ready to take her home.

On the way, she thought she saw Sam sleeping on a bench in the neighborhood playground. She decided to check in the morning to see if he was still there. Since he had no phone, that was her only way to communicate with him.

*****

On Wednesday, Dizzy left her house on foot shortly after seven o'clock and went straight to the playground. Luckily Sam was still there, packing his belongings. She greeted him.

"Good morning, Sam. I need to talk to you."

"I've also got something serious to tell you too. Can you sit for a minute?"

"No, I'm in a big hurry this morning. Marc has been very difficult lately, and I've got to be there to get him out of bed."

"Your job gets in the way."

"Don't start saying negative things about a job I love." She reflected for a minute. "Can you come and have dinner with me tomorrow?"

"Yes, ma'am."

Dizzy ignored his affected politeness and went her way. When she entered Marc's house, he was already up and feeding Devil in the kitchen.

"Hi, Dizzy. I've had a good time with Devil. Even my mom was playing with him last night."

"Are you ready for the show-and-tell next Wednesday?"

"Yeah, it will be fun, the kids will love it! Do you have to take Devil back home after the show?"

"Yes, I'd like to."

"Too bad! But I've got a second wish. You remember, before your trip?"

"That's right! Please tell me what's your other wish"

"Nope, it's still a secret. I'll tell you after the show-and-tell next week."

Dizzy didn't insist. She figured it would be good timing for Marc to tell her his secret when she took back her cat. She kept the little boy busy until his mother came home. Then she left without Devil.

When she got home, she felt lonely without her dear cat. Fortunately, her phone rang. She answered the call. To her surprise, a sweet childish voice came on. It was her granddaughter.

"Grandma, I got you. I'm so proud."

"Hi, Ruby, I mean Joy."

"Thanks for using my secret name."

"How did you get my phone number?"

"I looked it up in my mom's little book. But don't tell her, she doesn't want me to call you."

"I know."

"But I have the right to call my grandma! Anyway, I have a question for you."

"What is it?"

"You told me about the show-and-tell with your cat…"

"At Marc's school?"

"Yes. Can I take Devil to my school too? Please!"

"No, Joy. I decided your mom wouldn't like it."

"Because it's your cat? Too bad! OK, goodbye, Grandma."

Dizzy excused the six-year-old little girl for ending the phone call so abruptly. She was happy that Joy had called her for the first time. Hopefully their secret conversations would continue.

*****

On Thursday shortly after six o'clock, Dizzy's doorbell rang. It was Sam, dressed in blue pants and a matching windbreaker.

"I went to the Salvation Army again. They gave me these light hand-me-downs when I said I'm leaving for California this weekend…"

"Wait a minute. It turns out you can't leave this weekend. I wanted to tell you that I need Greenie for a few days."

"What's up? Going somewhere with another driver?"

She pretended not to have heard his innuendo. "I'd forgotten the show-and-tell with Devil next Wednesday at Marc's school. I need Greenie to transport my cat."

"No problem! I'll go a few days later. Is that all you wanted to tell me?" He looked straight into her in the eyes. "I've got some big news for you." He paused and said triumphantly. "I've been dry for one day."

"That's a good beginning! We'll have to celebrate."

"With pot," he said, making Dizzy uncomfortable.

They sat down on the floor in the living room and had some dinner. When she noticed Sam coming closer to her, she gently pushed him away and went to the kitchen under the pretext that they needed some water. Sam left shortly after dinner. Dizzy went to bed early.

*****

The next week, the show-and-tell with Devil at Marc's school turned out to be a huge success again. At the end of the event, the little boy looked triumphant. Dizzy, who attended the show in the morning, knew he was gaining more and more respect from his classmates. After the event, she went home with Devil.

That afternoon, as they were walking home after school, Marc confided in her. "My secret wish is to go to France soon. My cousin Nicolas called me to say he got a summer job far away from home. I really want to see him before that." His face became tense. "My mom can't go to France this year because of her new job. She won't let me go by myself, I'm sure."

"Have you discussed it with her?"

"No, it's a secret."

"I should talk to her about it. You think it's a good idea?"

"Please do!"

"I'll see what I can do." Dizzy resolved to talk to Chantal as soon as possible and made an appointment with her for the following day. She knew it would be good for the little boy's identity problems to have a visit with his cousin in the near future.

When Chantal came home the next day, she immediately sent her son to his room. The two women had a serious talk over coffee in the living room.

"Did Marc tell you about the wish he made before my trip?" Dizzy asked.

"No, he told me it was a secret."

"He told me about it yesterday. He would like to visit his cousin Nicolas in France before summer."

"Why so early?"

"Because his cousin will be away all summer." She paused. "Can you plan a short trip to France with Marc around his spring break at school?"

"Impossible. I promised to teach a special intensive class at that time." She reflected for a while. "I have a great idea. Maybe you can take Marc there."

"Me?"

"It would be good for him. He likes you very much. And I trust you totally."

"But…"

"Are you worried about the cost? Of course, I would pay for your expenses."

"It's not that, but I don't speak French."

"It is not a problem. Marc knows the language very well. He can help you."

Dizzy was tempted by this unexpected offer of a trip to France. It fitted her adventurous nature and insatiable curiosity. Besides, it would give the little boy self-confidence to act as her guide. She considered the wild proposal for a few minutes before accepting Chantal's offer. They agreed on a two-week-long trip around Marc's spring break.

The little boy, who had eavesdropped from his room, came out to hug the two women. After some chitchat about France, Dizzy left.

That evening, she had all kinds of thoughts about her upcoming trip to France: what to pack and what to do over there. She also worried about Devil: who would take care of him?

After listening to soothing New Age music in order to chase away all worries, her positive attitude took over again. She went to bed, determined to have a good time in France.

CHAPTER 11

The following week on Monday morning, when she arrived at Marc's house, Dizzy found a long note addressed to her on the kitchen table. Chantal wanted her to know she had called her sister in Paris on the weekend. Mireille, being used to Chantal's last-minute decisions about family visits to France, wasn't surprised by the sudden plan for Marc to visit before the summer. The little boy's mother had explained that he wanted to see his cousin before Nicolas left for his summer job. She had told Mireille that she couldn't not take the time off but that she didn't feel Marc was old enough to travel by himself, so he would be accompanied by his caretaker. Mireille had said that both of them would be welcome, having heard earlier of Dizzy's exceptionally good relationship with Marc.

The two sisters had tried to coordinate their respective sons' spring school breaks but weren't able to do so. Nicolas wouldn't be on vacation until Easter in mid-April, according to the French school calendar, and anyway he might spend his break in England to perfect his English. Chantal and Mireille then had agreed it would be best for Marc to visit France over his own spring break.

Dizzy felt pressured: things were happening too fast. The pressure increased on Monday afternoon when Chantal announced on her return from work that she had already discussed the tentative plan on the phone with her son's school principal. Marc's mother and the principal had agreed that the little boy could miss school for four days before spring break, which was due to start on Friday, March 22. Thus, Marc and his caretaker could leave for France the preceding weekend.

Dizzy panicked: it was under two weeks away. But Chantal reassured her.

"I am pretty sure that I can get airline tickets for Friday, March 15, before the big rush for spring break. It would be good for you and Marc to arrive in France on a Saturday morning. The traffic would be lighter from the airport to my sister's apartment in Paris."

"Can you get tickets for that day on such short notice?" Dizzy asked Chantal.

"Yes, I used to book our flights to Paris for our family visits at the last minute because of my husband's unpredictable work schedule." She teared up but continued in a firm voice. "In fact, I often got good prices for the tickets since the airlines want to fill up their planes at the last minute. Sometimes I paid for economy class, and they had us sitting in first class on the flight. Marc loved it, he got spoiled by the attendants."

It was obviously good for Chantal's emotional health to organize a trip to her native country. Dizzy started relaxing: after all, it wasn't in her hands. She joined the game of planning an international trip.

"You're an experienced traveler, Chantal. I trust you to get tickets at the last minute. But there's so little time for me to prepare for the trip!"

"What is it that you have to prepare?"

"First of all, I should find out if my passport is still valid. I got it to go to Germany when our oldest son and his family lived there for a while."

"When was that?"

"Let's see, my husband was already sick. Maybe three years ago."

"No problem. What else?"

"I've got to find someone to take care of Devil."

"How about that cat sitter you had when you went to the desert over Presidents' Day weekend?"

"That's right. I could ask her if she's free for those two weeks."

"Do not worry, all will go smoothly. You told me to get less anxious about everything. Now you are the one to worry."

Dizzy knew Chantal was right. Instead of rejoicing at an unexpected opportunity to discover Paris, she was worrying unnecessarily. She chided herself for her negative thoughts and quickly returned to her usual positive thinking. Most likely, the cat sitter would be available. If not, some other solution would come up. As for her recent promise to herself to slow down and start practicing yoga and meditation, that could wait for a few weeks.

"Thank you, Chantal, for putting me back on the right track. I was worrying too much. Life is to be enjoyed!"

"Yes, indeed. You always told me so when I was depressed, and it helped me a lot."

"Now you've become my helper!"

"I am glad to hear that. Planning a trip to France has always made me happy. I only wish that my dear husband was still alive."

"Is it the first time that Marc will go to France without you?" Dizzy asked, hoping to distract Chantal from her memories.

"Yes. It will be good for him. It will give him self-confidence. And he can discuss his identity problems with his cousin. Nicolas will understand."

After some chitchat about France, Dizzy said goodbye to Chantal and Marc and went home. She felt like relaxing with Devil for a while. She called the cat sitter who readily accepted the job for the second part of March.

Then Dizzy thought of other things to be done. She checked her passport, which indeed was still valid for a few years. Packing would be no problem, as she was always casual about clothing. In addition to a couple of pairs of slacks, she would also take a dress, just in case. She also made a mental note to take along a raincoat and an umbrella, Chantal having warned her about the uncertain weather in Paris at that time of year.

It occurred to Dizzy that she should tell her next-door neighbor about her planned absence. He could bring in the empty trash can after the garbage truck came and take care of her mail every day. However, she was hesitant due to the man's uncivil behavior on the day when she and her self-appointed botany teacher had intruded in his front yard. She decided to ask Sam for advice.

*****

111

The next morning, Dizzy took a chance and walked to the neighborhood park on her way to Marc's house. Luckily Sam was there. Without wondering why he had once again decided to spend the night there, she asked him to come to her house that evening and told him she had fresh news to share. He gladly accepted the invitation.

In the afternoon, Chantal on her return from work declared triumphantly that she had gotten two airline tickets from Portland to Paris for Friday, March 15. Dizzy tried to calm down while walking home.

At six o'clock, she heard the doorbell. It was Sam, dressed in his best clothes. He tried to kiss her on the lips, but she gently pushed him away.

"Don't, Sam. We're just friends."

"But I can't help being attracted to you, Dizzy. Haven't you wondered why I sleep in the park nearby, instead of the men's shelter or under the bridge? I want to be close to you. You're my savior."

"Your savior?"

"You saved my life."

"Me?"

"You and Sunbeam help me so much to pull me out of my drinking problem!"

Dizzy had come across addicts in her long nursing career, and she knew that they have to decide themselves to quit abusing alcohol or drugs. But she was glad she could be of some help to Sam as a friend. She started feeling guilty about leaving him so soon. It was high time to tell him about her impending trip to France.

Sam didn't express any surprise, probably because he knew by then that Dizzy was adventurous and impulsive. He immediately made her an offer.

"I could take care of Devil."

"But you'll be at the commune with Sunbeam. It's very important that you get help from him. I hired a cat sitter for Devil."

"Why would you do that? I could come back from the commune."

DIZZY'S JOIE DE VIVRE

"I've got an idea. How would you like to live in my house while I'm gone? That way, I wouldn't have to ask my next-door neighbor to take my mail in."

"It's a deal! I could go see Sunbeam for a few days to set up some dates for playing music in bars and come back just before you leave."

"Good planning. I'll cancel the cat sitter right away."

"I forgot, do you need Greenie just now?"

"That's the last thing I need," Dizzy said laughing. "You can have her right now."

She went to the kitchen and prepared something simple to eat for dinner. They ate seated, as usual, on the living room floor and drank tea from the only cup she owned. As they took turns sipping tea, Sam pulled his pipe from his pocket, filled it with pot, lit it, and handed it to Dizzy. At first, she refused, but she was feeling restless after so many quick decisions. She took the pipe and began inhaling. She had learned in no time to enjoy the calming effects of pot.

Suddenly, they heard a loud knock on the front door. Sam got up and went to see who it was. He cautiously opened the door and Denise barged in, dressed informally in sports clothes. Dizzy quickly extinguished the pipe, expecting trouble since her daughter-in-law never came to visit.

"Hello, Denise," Dizzy said softly.

"Hi. I smell something funny. What did you cook?"

"Nothing special."

"Who is this young man?"

"My driver. I told you about him."

"Anyway, I've come to order you not to call our daughter ever again."

"But I didn't call her..."

"I know. It was Ruby that called you. I found my little book with a post-it marking the page with your number. She had forgotten to remove it. I confronted her about it, and she confessed to having used my little book to call you." Denise caught her breath and continued dramatically. "I forbid you to ever call her or answer any calls from her. You're such a bad influence on our young daughter! Like eating in a disgusting way. Look at you, sitting on the floor just now to eat dinner, like a savage. And that funny smell." She pinched her nose and continued in a solemn tone of voice. "Anyway, I made sure Ruby won't call you. I warned her the punishment would be severe. And I'll find a more decent babysitter for her."

Dizzy was horrified. It was bad enough to be forbidden to see her granddaughter or communicate with her. Being told she was a bad influence on a young child hurt even more. All she wanted was to share her enjoyment of life with the little girl and teach her how to be a free spirit.

Sam lit up the pipe again and handed it to Dizzy. Denise exploded. "You smoke pot now! I was wondering about the smell when I came in. Now I recognize it."

"That means you're a pot user yourself," Sam said teasingly.

"Not me, for heaven's sake. But our neighbors often smoke pot, and sometimes the wind blows the smell our way. Once we invited our church minister for dinner. It was a warm summer night, so we sat in the backyard. The neighbors were sitting outside smoking pot, and our minister looked like he wanted to join them…"

"You see, your minister appreciates it," Sam said sarcastically.

"But he's young. Not like my mother-in-law." Denise paused. "She's a shameless lady. At her age, she shouldn't do things like that."

"There's no age for fun," Dizzy said cheerfully.

Denise was mortified, feeling that she had lost control of the situation. She switched to a different topic. "And that horrible car in your driveway, when will you get rid of it?"

"Why do you want her to get rid of it?" Sam asked, staring at Denise.

"I like my green car," Dizzy chimed in. "Anyway, I told Sam he could use it to go on a trip tomorrow."

Denise exploded and looked down at her mother-in-law on the floor. "What? Are you crazy? Lending your car to that drifter?"

"You're crazy yourself," Sam shouted, standing up. "Get out of here!"

"Are you threatening me? I'll call the police."

"Go ahead!"

"The cops will see you and Dizzy are smoking pot."

"So what? It's legal in Oregon now," Sam said calmly.

At that point, Denise realized she was definitely losing the fight. Enraged, she stormed out without saying a word, slamming the front door.

"Good riddance!" Dizzy said. But deep inside she was sad about the tense family situation.

Sam lit up the pipe again. They shared it in silence, still sitting on the floor. Once the "shameless elderly lady" felt relaxed again, she asked Sam to leave. She went to fetch the car key and handed it to him with a $50 bill "for gas." He left without trying to kiss her or even come close to her. Later, she heard him start the car engine. He was gone after a few minutes. She felt strangely lonely and went to bed early.

*****

On Saturday morning, as Dizzy was looking forward to a quiet day in Devil's company after a tumultuous week, her phone rang a little after nine. It was Julian.

"Hi, Mom. Are you going to be home today?"

"Yes, today's Saturday, so I don't have to take care of Marc."

"Who's Marc?"

"The little boy I help on school days. By the way, I'm very excited. I'm going to France with him in a couple of…"

"Listen, I don't have time to listen to your stories just now. A client is due in two minutes in my office. Can we talk later? I could come by at eleven fifteen. I'm showing a house at ten thirty close to your place and another one at eleven forty-five in the same part of town."

"OK, see you at eleven fifteen."

Dizzy put down her iPhone and sighed. This visit by her son between two business appointments would be too short for her taste. When would Julian have time for a real visit with his mother? She shrugged her shoulders and took Devil in her arms. He purred as she kept petting him and talking to him.

"Babe, you're like me. We both take time to enjoy life. Some people are too busy making money."

She flashed back to her memories of Julian as a young man. He was a carefree and altruistic student of philosophy until he met Denise, a business major. He started dating her, fascinated by her New York superficial sophistication, and he changed drastically within a few months. Under her influence, he switched from philosophy to business studies with focus on real estate. After they got married, he became a successful realtor, pushed by his ambitious and spendthrift wife who needed a great deal of money for her extravagant tastes.

Dizzy heard Julian park his car in the driveway at exactly eleven fifteen. She opened the front door and welcomed him in a joking fashion.

"Hello, Julian. You didn't give me the pleasure of scolding my little boy for being late."

"Hello, Mom. I'm sure you know punctuality is essential in my kind of business," he answered in a serious tone of voice, hugging her absentmindedly.

He inspected the living room with a critical look. "How bare! I couldn't stand it."

"To each his own, I like it this way," Dizzy said laughingly. She brought the lone chair from the kitchen for her son and sat down on the living room floor.

"By the way, did you get rid of your car?" Julian asked after a moment of embarrassing silence. "I didn't see it in the driveway. Sold it to someone? For how much?"

"No, I lent it to a friend."

"The man that was here on Tuesday evening? Denise told me about him. She described him to me. I bet he's the same guy I saw in the playground a while back. Beware, Mom, that drifter's after your money."

"How can you say that about someone you don't even know?" Dizzy asked angrily.

"Anyway, what I came to tell you is to leave my wife alone! Denise told me you were rude to her a couple of days. And that bum was even worse."

"She was hysterical and threatened to call the cops."

"She had a reason for that. You were smoking pot in the company of a drifter. She wanted the cops to arrest him."

"Smoking pot is legal now in Oregon. Besides, I don't need protection from anyone," Dizzy said defiantly.

"Who is that man? Tell me!"

"He's my driver. He drove my car on our trip to the Mojave Desert."

"A lady your age shouldn't be running around with a guy half her age."

"Why not?'

"People might think he's your lover, a gigolo."

"I don't care what people think."

"But I do. My clients are decent people. They might hear about my shameless mom. I want you to get rid of that weirdo."

"You have no right."

"Where is he? I want to talk to him."

"He's on his way to visit your Uncle Sunbeam, I mean Adam," Dizzy said calmly.

"Uncle Adam? He's a madman. You told me he lives in a commune."

"So what?" She giggled and became mischievous. "Do you know what a commune is? It's a place where the people are free spirits and share everything. It's a place where kids learn through experience to feel close to nature and animals." After a while, she asked her son a question. "Can you guess why your Uncle Adam's commune is called Crazy Bear?"

"No idea," Julian said, yawning.

"I found out the kids gave the name Crazy Bear to a cute bear they see every day. And the grownups adopted the name for their commune. I saw that resident bear roaming around."

"You went there? With that guy?"

"Yes. By the way Adam changed his name to Sunbeam. He and my driver Sam became instant pals. They're going to play music together in bars down there, and Sunbeam wants to help Sam overcome his drinking problem."

"Good luck!" Julian said sarcastically.

"Why are you so negative? You should have faith in people when they want to reform."

"Please don't lecture, Mom." Julian yawned again and looked at his gold watch. "I have to go. My next appointment…"

He left hurriedly, without saying goodbye or hugging his mother. Dizzy heard his car racing down the street. She found Devil lying on her bed and confided in him.

"Poor Julian, my little boy isn't happy. I wish I could do something for him. Too bad he isn't ready to share my joyfulness." She reflected for a while "Oh, I forgot to finish telling him about my trip to France. I'll have to call him. At his office, not at his home. I don't want to speak to Denise. She wears me down, and I can't do anything for her."

Dizzy called Julian at about five o'clock and found him still at the office.

"Hello, Julian. It's me, Mom."

"Hello, Mom. Good timing, I just finished working on some papers. I made a sale this afternoon, Denise will be happy."

"Poor you, working so hard!"

"I enjoy working hard. It makes me forget the problems at home."

"Problems at home?"

"Never mind!" He kept silent for a few seconds and changed the subject. "You wanted to tell me something important…"

"I'm going to France next week," Dizzy said excitedly.

"With that drifter?"

"No, with Marc, the little boy I watch on weekdays."

"How come?"

"He wanted to go before the summer to see his French relatives, and his mother can't go because of her job. She asked me to take him there over his spring break. We're going to stay with Marc's aunt and his cousin for about two weeks."

"Congratulations!" He paused for a little while. "Listen, I have to go. Denise and I are going out for dinner tonight."

"Another business dinner?" Dizzy couldn't help teasing her son.

"Yes, and we hired a babysitter," Julian teased back. "Good night, Mom."

"Good evening, Julian."

Dizzy remained pensive for a while, phone in hand. What could be the problems to which her son had alluded? She thought of marital problems, Denise being such a difficult person! But she decided to defeat negative thinking since she could do nothing about her son's problems. She grabbed her ukulele and played a couple of songs.

Later, Dizzy went to the kitchen to feed Devil and to make dinner for herself. After dinner, she returned to the living room and put on a CD, *Scheherazade* by Rimsky-Korsakov. The barefoot eighty-year-old woman started dancing exuberantly along with the music, feeling happy again at the thought of her trip to France. She was determined to have fun in Paris!

CHAPTER 12

After thinking about the sightseeing she would like to do in Paris, Dizzy felt more prepared for her trip. She had drawn up a tentative list of Paris sites to visit and gotten information about them online. Also, she felt calmer after getting a call from her brother reporting that Sam had arrived at the commune in northern California.

On Monday afternoon, Dizzy read her Paris sightseeing list to Marc: the Eiffel Tower, Notre-Dame de Paris, Montmartre, Tour Montparnasse, and a few well-known museums. The little boy laughed, looking blasé, and called her a typical tourist. "I know most of these places. You can go by yourself. They speak English there."

"Good! But you don't seem to like Paris very much."

"We go there every year. Even in summer, it's too crowded, and my aunt's apartment is really small. I like her house in Brittany better."

"Why?"

"It's a lot bigger, and it has a yard. At least their apartment in Paris is on the top floor, and there is a big terrace with potted flowers and bushes." Dizzy made a mental note of Marc's growing interest in plants.

As the seven-year-old boy got more and more excited about their upcoming trip, he became more difficult to handle, and Dizzy thought of calming activities related to nature. She got him a book with beautiful illustrations of trees around the world, *The hidden life of trees*, by Peter Wohlleben.

Dizzy and Marc spent some time looking at the book together. She asked the little boy to choose his favorite picture, and he selected one representing colorful red maple trees from British Columbia. It reminded them that red maples in their own area should already be budding out.

The next day, on their walks to and from school, they did notice buds on maple trees. Dizzy invented a new game: the two of them would compete to be the first one to identify a budding tree, and the winner would get to make a secret wish. A few minutes later, she pointed out a tree to Marc. "I see some buds on this silver maple tree."

"You saw it first, Dizzy, so you can make a wish, a secret one."

"OK." She secretly made a wish to do something adventurous in Paris.

"Look! I see yellow bells!" Marc said excitedly.

"That's forsythia," said his self-appointed botany teacher.

"I didn't know the name. Can I still make a wish?'

"Go ahead." Marc made a secret wish that his French aunt would take them to Brittany during their stay in France.

A little later, he and Dizzy saw exquisite pink camellia blossoms at the very same time and decided there was no winner that time. The competitive game ended, but they continued enjoying the sight of budding magnolia trees and the sounds of chirping birds announcing the arrival of spring.

As the date of their departure approached, Marc had calmed down, thanks to Dizzy's creativeness. She felt fulfilled for having shared more of her enjoyment of beauty with the little boy. That was another important ingredient of her joie de vivre, and she knew that children learn to appreciate plants through education and experience. She resolved to continue being imaginative and to devise more activities related to nature for Marc.

*****

On Wednesday evening, as Dizzy was reflecting on the past few days, her phone rang. It was her son.

"Hi, Mom. This is Julian."

"I still recognize your voice," she said impatiently, surprised he would call again so soon. She became sarcastic. "Do you want me to watch Joy, I mean Ruby, next time you go out?"

"Mom, stop teasing me, it's a serious situation." He cleared his throat. "Denise kicked me out last night."

"What?"

"I said Denise kicked me out last night." His voice faltered. "I'm calling from my office. She doesn't want me in the house."

"What happened?"

"Yesterday we went to a business dinner." He sighed and then blurted out angrily. "What happened is that Denise kept flirting with a banker the whole evening. I confronted her about it last night. At first, she denied everything, but I forced her to tell me the truth. It turns out she's been having an affair with that banker for a few months. According to her, he'll help secure a loan from his bank for her to open up a jewelry store. That guy wants her to move with him eventually. For now, she and Ruby will stay in our home, but she kicked me out and says she wants a divorce." He started sobbing.

"Poor baby! Where are you going to live?"

"I'm staying at a hotel downtown…"

"It must be lonely." Dizzy's heart immediately went out to her prodigal son. She was ready to forgive him for having become a stranger for so many years. "Come on over, Julian!" She looked at the time on her phone: it was six thirty. He probably hadn't eaten dinner yet. "Do you want to have dinner with me? I usually eat around seven."

Julian readily accepted the invitation. He obviously hated the idea of being by himself in the evening. Dizzy turned off her phone and rushed to the kitchen to prepare a barley soup, one of her son's favorite dishes when he was growing up in the family home.

A few minutes before seven o'clock, she heard a car in the driveway. "The door's open, Julian. Come on in!" Dizzy said as cheerfully as possible. She saw that her son carried a large Papa Murphy's pizza box in his hands.

"What's that?"

"I got a pepperoni pizza for dinner. It used to be your favorite."

"But I've become a vegetarian. You know, I like to reinvent myself once in a while."

"Crazy," Julian said sotto voce so that his mother wouldn't hear. "Oh well, more pizza for me," he said in a falsely cheerful tone of voice. "But what will you have?"

"I made a barley soup, your favorite dish..."

"I'll join you. I can reheat the pizza in the microwave oven at the hotel for another meal."

He put the pizza box on a counter in the kitchen, and the two of them hugged each other in a long tight embrace. Dizzy remarked that he looked tired and he told her he hadn't slept well the previous night, being angry with Denise and concerned about his family's future. Also, he complained that sometimes it got noisy at the downtown hotel. She suggested he stay at her place overnight. He looked around and declined.

"I'm sorry, Mom, but it's too bare for me here." He immediately realized he must have hurt her feelings and quickly changed the topic. "I'm getting hungry, let's eat."

Dizzy poured the barley soup into her only bowl and grabbed her single big spoon. He followed her to the living room where she sat down on the floor. It took him a couple of minutes to do the same.

"You start," Dizzy said in a natural tone of voice, handing the bowl of soup and the spoon to Julian. He tried a spoonful of the soup and smacked his lips.

'Good, Mom, you sure know how to make my favorite soup. I haven't had it in years. Denise never made barley soup. She says it's too difficult."

"It's very simple."

"But Denise doesn't want to spend much time in the kitchen. She prefers to go shopping."

"She's a consumerist, no question about that."

"What's wrong with that? Let's not be too critical of her." He stopped eating. "At least, our house looked nice."

"Not like here. Go ahead, say what you think, son!"

"Mom, I didn't mean that. You're free to do what you want in your own home."

"I should hope so!" She looked angrily at Julian. "But you don't like it here. I bet you don't like having to sit on the floor to eat dinner. You don't like sharing my only soup bowl and spoon I have. And you don't like my bare living room."

"Don't get upset, Mom. It's hard for me to switch from Denise's sophisticated ways to your, whatever you can call it."

"Downsizing, it's called, or decluttering. You know, your father was a hoarder, a pack rat all his life. I suffered through it, but deep down I'm a minimalist. I want to live without baggage. It's good to have just a few possessions, you feel lighter."

"You're too extreme, Mom."

"And you've become too attached to material things. You're too greedy for money. You work too hard."

"I have to, for Denise's needs."

"But now you won't have to do that."

"Are you kidding? Denise is a demanding person and greedy for money. I'm sure she'll claim alimony in addition to child support. In the best-case scenario, she'll be able to open a jewelry store with that banker's help and make money. In the worst-case scenario, I'll have to support her and Ruby. It means making even more money all my working life. What a grim future!"

"Don't catastrophize, it's bad for your health! You've got to come to terms with your new reality. You're a different person now. You're starting a new chapter of life."

"That's easy for you to say."

"Think of it this way. Once in a while you should reinvent yourself. The way flowers renew themselves every season. Forget the past and the uncertain future. Live in the present!"

Dizzy stopped lecturing her son but caught herself thinking of Sam and his contagious carefree, happy-go-lucky attitude. After the homeless man's initial surprise at her bare home, he had proved to be flexible and had behaved like a real trooper. He seemed not to mind her minimalist ways.

She came out of her reverie when she heard Julian's car speed out of the driveway. It reminded her of the speeding car that had killed a cat a while ago. She went to the kitchen to check on Devil.

He looked fine, but there was no pepperoni pizza on the counter. Her son must have taken it to the hotel to heat up in the microwave oven, instead of enjoying her homemade barley soup.

Dizzy shrugged her shoulders. She was both sad and relieved that Julian had left. An argument with her son was the last thing she wanted. Better to leave him alone! He was obviously suffering and angry, but he would eventually turn around. All evening, she clung to her optimistic outlook about her favorite child.

*****

It didn't take long for Dizzy's "hands-off" attitude and positive thinking to bear fruit. Julian called her two hours later and proceeded to summarize his most recent conversation with Denise about parental visiting rights. He and his future ex-wife had agreed Ruby could visit him every weekend, which would give the new couple some privacy or occasionally let them go on a trip. The plan would start the next weekend. Julian asked his mother to help him take care of the child when she returned from France, since weekends were particularly busy for a realtor. Dizzy couldn't help feeling victorious: she would start seeing her granddaughter regularly, despite Denise's orders to the contrary! She quickly assured her son that he could count on her for childcare, whenever his job kept him busy on the weekend.

She heard Julian's office phone ring in the background, and they hurriedly said goodbye. Dizzy couldn't wait to invent a little song about her granddaughter and Devil, which she played on her ukulele, singing loudly. It went like this:

> *Once upon a time,*
> *there were a little girl called Joy*
> *and an orange cat called Devil.*
> *They played together for hours,*
> *and when she petted him*
> *he would purr contentedly.*
> *They really loved each other*
> *And were very good playmates.*

The eighty-year-old grandmother was dancing around the living room when she suddenly stopped. Lightning had struck. What if Julian would agree to housesit and cat-sit during her two-week absence? It would give her son a place to entertain his daughter as soon as the next weekend.

It occurred to Dizzy that she should discuss her idea with Sam, who was due to return in a few days to housesit and cat-sit for her. But he didn't have a phone. What to do? She decided it wasn't too late to call her brother. By chance, he answered right away.

"Hello, Sis."

"How did you know it was me?"

Sunbeam teased his sister. "Do you have Alzheimer's now? You should know the caller's name shows up on an iPhone."

"I forgot. It's still new to me. At age eighty, I've got to learn so many new things!"

"Me too!" They both laughed.

"Anyway, I'm calling about Sam. I need to talk to him tonight."

"Let me tell you, he's doing very well. We've become real buddies. He goes to Alcoholics Anonymous with me, and there's no alcohol at Crazy Bear, as you know. And when we get gigs in a bar, he drinks tomato juice."

"That's nice, but can you find him right away and lend him your phone? I've got something important to ask him."

"I'll go and get him."

Dizzy got nervous. What if Sam was counting on the chance to live in a real home for two weeks? Also, would he mind being deprived of two weeks alone with Devil? She chased away these misgivings when she heard her brother on the phone. "I found Sam playing music," Sunbeam said. "I'll give him my phone to talk to you. Here's Sam."

"Hello, Dizzy. Sunbeam told me you've got something important to tell me."

"Yes, it's about the housesitting and cat-sitting while I'm gone." She spoke nervously, being afraid that Sam wouldn't like the change of plans. "You were going to return just before I leave for France. What happens is that my youngest son is getting a divorce. His wife kicked him out, and the poor baby is staying in some hotel downtown. He doesn't like it, and I thought…"

"You want for him to stay in your house for a while?"

"How did you guess?"

"Easy. You're so nice, always helping other people!" He sighed. "That's why I like you. You do a really good job sharing your love of life with lost people like me."

Dizzy didn't not reply, since she didn't care for his puppy love. She put him back on the right track. "Would it be OK with you if my son stays in my house for now? He'd take care of Devil while I'm in France."

"You do what you want." He paused and resumed speaking in a resolute tone of voice. "Anyway, I'd like to stay at Crazy Bear for now. Sunbeam is helping me get rid of my drinking problem. And we make good music together." He reflected for a few seconds. "But what about Greenie?"

"I really don't have any use for her. My son has a car, in case I need a ride."

"We talked about another trip to the desert…"

"Let's talk about that later. I live in the present."

Dizzy was in a hurry to invite her son to move in. After thanking Sam for his flexibility, she hurriedly said goodbye to him. He said goodbye too, sounding sorry to put a quick end to their conversation. For once she was insensitive to his feelings: Julian and Joy came first for her just now.

Dizzy had to put her new plan into action without delay. She called back her son and told him he could stay in her house as long as he wanted, pointing out that he would be also good for his daughter on weekends. She also told Julian that the spare bedroom had a huge closet in which he could hang his clothes. He accepted readily, saying that he would bring some essentials the next day after work and have dinner with her.

It had been an exhausting day, with so much making and changing plans practically at the last minute. Dizzy thought to herself that she generally liked change, but not this fast! Now she wanted to focus on her trip.

She turned on her computer and went to websites giving information about France, particularly Paris. She happened to find an article titled *The ten Paris streets you have to walk down*, with pictures of those streets. Being a regular walker, the first sentence of the article caught her attention: "Paris is best explored on foot." She made notes about the streets listed in the article, particularly *Rue Montorgueil* because the article showed a picture of an interesting outdoor market there.

She also checked another website that had information about red poppies. It listed a place close to Paris where wildflowers were returning to the fields, thanks to bio agricultural methods. Dizzy, being an eternal educator, made a mental note to take Marc there.

*****

On Thursday, Marc was, not surprisingly, difficult to handle. His mother and Dizzy excused his behavior because they knew he was impatient to go to Paris and see his cousin.

Also, he expressed concern about Devil. Who would be taking care of the cat in his mama's absence? Dizzy assured the little boy that everything was planned, without giving him the details. Informing the seven-year-old child of the complicated plan would only serve to make him anxious, especially the presence of her granddaughter in the house on weekends. Would a six-year-old little girl think of keeping the front door closed to prevent Devil from running away?

In the evening, Julian came to his mother's house as planned. This time he hadn't gotten pepperoni pizza, but vegetarian Indian food. After coming in, he put down the containers on a kitchen counter and went to unload his car. He brought in two folding beds and positioned them in the spare bedroom. He also brought tons of clothing. His mother teased him.

"Why so many suits?"

"My clown outfits on work days. Do you want me to look like a homeless guy when I show houses to my clients?" He laughed at his own jokes, but Dizzy did not appreciate them, thinking that they were tasteless, particularly the second one.

She went to the kitchen and put the Indian food on paper plates. She hadn't ventured to make barley soup this time, since a few days ago, Julian had left without eating much of his favorite dish, lovingly prepared by his mother.

They had dinner seated on the floor in the living room, passing around the paper plates and the only fork she owned. This time Julian didn't seem to mind his mother's unconventional ways. At least he didn't make critical comments or behave rudely. After all, his mom was rescuing him from his desperate loneliness at the hotel. Moreover, she had thought up an excellent solution for his daughter's weekend visits.

After dinner, Dizzy handed a house key to Julian, and they spent some time going over instructions about the house and Devil. She repeatedly told her son to be extremely careful to keep the front door closed at all times: if not, her indoor cat might escape, since he was very curious about the outside world. She also gave Julian the name and phone number of a reliable caretaker named Liliana for her granddaughter. The busy realtor would need someone to take care of his daughter on the weekend when at work.

Shortly after eight o'clock, Dizzy and her son wished each other a good night and retired to their respective bedrooms. She still had some packing to do, and it wasn't a good evening to be a night owl. Chantal and Marc were due at her house at seven the next morning to leave for the Portland airport.

CHAPTER 13

At the Portland airport, Marc's mother took charge, being an experienced international traveler. After Dizzy and the little boy checked in and left their two small suitcases at the United Airlines counter, Chantal led them to the security area where they had to part. She kissed her son affectionately, hugged Dizzy, and wished them "Bon voyage." Once they had gone through the security checkpoint, she waved to them goodbye and left the airport.

Dizzy was now in charge of the child, which made her nervous for the first time. She held Marc's hand tightly on the way to the departure gates, not knowing who was guiding whom. The little boy seemed to be so much at home in the airport! He obviously knew it better than she did. Pretty soon he would be acting as her personal guide in France, having been there several times and speaking the language. That was a strange role reversal for his caretaker, but she turned it into a new adventure: an elderly lady being led by a seven-year-old chaperone.

After they reached their departure gate, Dizzy realized they would have a long wait before boarding, and she would have to keep Marc occupied. The parade of international passengers gave her an idea. The little boy would have to try to guess the travelers' origins on the basis of their clothing, manners, and language. He quickly identified a family of American Sikh Indians because of the men's turbans, as well as a tight group of Japanese students speaking their own language. But he put an end to the game when he noticed a young woman wearing a colorful dress and carrying a baby on her back in a piece of matching cloth.

"I bet she's from Africa, where I'm from," Marc whispered in Dizzy's ear. It made her think that the little boy's identity problem was still very much on his mind. Hopefully, his cousin Nicolas would help him come to terms with the issue.

After embarking on the first leg of their trip, Marc got busy working on the coloring books that an attendant had given him, and Dizzy started to relax. From her window seat, she could see the beautiful snowy mountains of Oregon. While flying over northern California, she fleetingly thought of Sam's infatuation for her and felt relieved that her son was the one staying in her house. Everything was falling into place, with Joy due to visit her father every weekend. Dizzy was elated.

She and Marc had to transfer to another plane in San Francisco. The passengers that the little boy had quickly identified in the Portland airport were all going on the same flight to Paris.

After boarding the plane for the international flight in the afternoon, they settled into their seats for the long haul. When they were offered beverages, Marc chose a soda pop while Dizzy ordered a scotch whiskey on the rocks. She wanted to drink some good scotch whiskey in order to erase the memory of the ordinary bourbon she had drunk with Sam on their first encounter. Being more used to wine, she got slightly drunk again.

When she heard pop music coming from Marc's earphones, she turned on the classical music station on her own headset. They were playing Beethoven's Ninth Symphony, one of her favorite pieces. She impulsively stood up and started marking the tempo with her arms, like an orchestra conductor. Embarrassed, Marc tried to get her to calm her down. "Stop it, Dizzy. People are looking at you."

"Who cares? I'm so excited to go to Paris!"

A grouchy middle-aged female passenger came to reprimand her, saying that an elderly lady like her shouldn't create a spectacle, and Dizzy sat down in order to avoid embarrassing Marc any longer.

A few minutes later, they were served first when the food cart rolled down the aisle. "You see, Marc, we got lunch before everyone else, probably because of my behavior," Dizzy remarked.

"Good, I was getting really hungry."

"I bet the attendants wanted to keep us busy. I'm glad I did that, we got rewarded." She laughed. It felt good to share her free spiritedness with the little boy.

They ate their lunch in silence, and the rest of the afternoon both Dizzy and Marc took long naps. When they finally woke up, it was already dark on the east coast, the plane having crossed three time zones. More drinks and food were served, and then everyone settled down with pillows and blankets for the short night.

The plane landed at the General de Gaulle airport on Saturday in the late morning. After a few hours of sleep, Dizzy felt alert, knowing that she had to be in charge. Chantal's sister and her seventeen-year-old son were waiting for them but wouldn't be able to meet them until the travelers claimed their luggage and went through some formalities. So Marc and his caretaker followed the other passengers to the baggage claim.

Suddenly, a large group of Japanese travelers appeared. Dizzy was distracted by Marc's remark that they looked like the Japanese students they had seen in the Portland airport. Holding the little boy by the hand, she started following the wrong Japanese group to go to the carousels.

A few minutes later, an announcement in French came over the loudspeaker. Marc translated it without waiting for the same announcement in English: two suitcases coming from San Francisco had been found abandoned in the baggage area, and they would be detonated if the owners did not claim them immediately. Dizzy realized that they were at the wrong carousel and ran to recover their luggage. She had forgotten that France had been forced to establish strict anti-terrorism rules in places like airports.

After getting their suitcases just in time, Dizzy shouted triumphantly, "We got our luggage!" A few heads turned, but she didn't care. Then she and Marc went through police and customs formalities. Finally, they met Nicolas and his mother who welcomed them warmly and led them to the parking lot, carrying the two rescued suitcases.

On the way from the Roissy airport (the common French name, Dizzy quickly learned), Mireille, who spoke only little English but understood it, concentrated on her driving. Meanwhile the two cousins, obviously thrilled to be together, engaged in a lively conversation in English. Nicolas spoke it fairly well, with a British accent, which French schools usually prefer to any American accent.

As they were stopped at a traffic light in Paris, Marc noticed Dizzy looking at a huge sign indicating *Pas de porte à vendre*. He proudly translated for her.

"That sign says 'No door for sale'…. Silly sign, right, Nicolas, if they don't have any doors for sale?"

"I hate to tell you, stupid, *pas de porte* means 'storefront' in this case. We'd better send you back where you came from!"

They both roared with laughter at that racist innuendo. Dizzy was happy to see that Nicolas could deal with identity problems in a humorous fashion. Marc obviously understood and appreciated his older cousin's sense of humor, as there was clearly a special connection between the two of them.

When they arrived at Mireille's top-floor apartment, Nicolas gave Dizzy a tour. His single mother couldn't afford to rent a more modern apartment. All the rooms in her relatively old apartment were small by American standards. But Dizzy immediately fell in love with the large terrace. It had an expansive view of Paris, including all the places she wanted to visit, and lots of potted plants, as Marc had told her earlier. She planned to spend as much time on the terrace as the early spring weather would allow.

Dizzy was surprised to discover that the French often keep their bedroom doors closed. Another surprising thing for her in the apartment was that the restroom was separate from the bathroom. It would take her several days to go to the right place.

Mireille had prepared a light dinner to be eaten on a folding table in the living room. But the travelers weren't hungry and wanted to go to bed early. Before retiring to the guest room, where two twin beds were ready for them, Dizzy and Marc had a conversation with their hosts. Nicolas told them in English that his mother planned to take them all to Brittany for a few days. Marc jumped with joy when he heard that his secret wish would be fulfilled. He was also happy to hear that it was up to him and his cousin to plan activities on the next day for the two of them.

*****

133

On Sunday morning, Dizzy woke up to the sound of church bells. Mireille had set up a simple breakfast on a tiny table in the kitchen. The two women and two boys took turns eating slices of bread covered with jam or Nutella and drinking coffee or hot chocolate. That was light fare for the Americans, but Marc whispered in Dizzy's ear that lunch was the most important meal of the day for the French.

After breakfast, the two boys decided to go to the Champ de Mars at the foot of the Eiffel Tower, a hot spot for riding scooters. They were planning to rent electric scooters there. Mireille gave some money to Nicolas for the rental fee. She also asked her son to tell Dizzy in English about Notre-Dame de Paris.

Although nonreligious, Mireille liked to go to the Cathedral on Sunday morning for High Mass, when the organist usually played glorious music on the exceptional organ. She wanted Dizzy to come along. After the religious service, she would be able to show her the art treasures in the church. Also, because of her secretarial job in a government office, the French lady had permission to access special parts of the cathedral where ordinary citizens were not allowed to go.

Dizzy gratefully accepted Mireille's offer to spend part of the day in Notre-Dame, on the condition that lunch would be on her. They dressed elegantly and went to the cathedral on the subway, arriving in time for High Mass. The organ music was sublime, and they then toured the cathedral in the late morning. In spite of the crowds of tourists, they were able to admire in particular the superb stained glass windows.

When they saw the long lines outside to get to the top of the church, they decided it was time for lunch. Luckily, Mireille knew how to avoid tourist traps, and she led Dizzy to an authentic *bistrot*. They had an omelet and ratatouille, accompanied by a basketful of slices of baguette. After their *café gourmand*—a plate of small pastries with a demitasse of express coffee—they returned to Notre-Dame. They valiantly climbed the many narrow steps to the top and, surrounded by gargoyles, admired the view of the Seine with its multiple bridges.

Then Mireille talked to one of the guards and presented her permit to enter the *forêt*, as the French call the wooden beams that support the whole church, including the spire. There, Dizzy was greeted by the surreal scene of numerous beams carved in centuries-old oak trees.[1]

Around six o'clock, Mireille said it was time to go home and prepare dinner, but Dizzy wanted to stay in Notre-Dame a little longer. Once her personal guide had left, she sat down on a chair in a remote corner of the church near the stained glass window that she had liked best. As the tourists gradually left, it got quieter and quieter. At first Dizzy enjoyed the silence, but after a while, she dozed off, still being jet lagged from her trip. Sleeping soundly, she didn't hear the announcement later in the evening that the doors were closing for the day.

When she woke up after a long nap, she discovered that all of the church doors were locked, and she was alone in the church. She tried desperately to get out, banging on the doors and calling for help. Nobody heard her, and she had unfortunately left her iPhone in Mireille's apartment.

After panicking at the thought of having to spend the whole night in the church, she resigned herself to the situation and turned her misfortune into a positive event. Was this the Paris adventure she had secretly wished for? She started inventing different characters for herself. First she imagined she was a fairy with a magic wand that would miraculously open the doors. She tried in vain to do so, using a big candle as her magic wand. Then she thought of herself as a warrior; she would get into yoga poses called Warrior Two or Warrior Three and would fight an imaginary enemy with the big candle as a sword. But nothing worked.

Finally, she gave up and prepared a bed for herself, using three chairs. She lay down on them, thinking it would make up a good story to tell Marc. She went to sleep with her jacket draped over her and dreamed of holding Devil in her arms.

*****

---

[1] Author's note. The account of Dizzy's visit to Notre-Dame de Paris was written before the catastrophic fire that ravaged the cathedral on April 15, 2019. According to the chronology I created for my novel, Dizzy would have visited the world-renowned church just a few weeks before the fire.

The next morning, she heard a guard opening the front door with a noisy key. She got up, ready to explain her presence in the church.

"My name is Dizzy. I got locked in here last night."

He stared at her in disbelief and spoke to her in French. She didn't understand, and he continued in broken English.

"The gargoyles, they tried catch you?"

Dizzy laughed at the guard's joke. But she was in a hurry to get out and go "home" to reassure Marc and his French relatives that she was OK. Luckily, she found a few euros in her purse, hailed a cab, and fifteen minutes later arrived at Mireille's apartment.

They had called the police on Sunday night, to no avail, and were greatly relieved that she was alive and well. They hugged her warmly, and she proceeded to tell them what had happened to her, cheerfully turning her misfortune into an amusing story. After a while, Mireille had to go to work and Nicolas left for school, since it was Monday.

Once Dizzy and Marc were alone in the apartment, they held each other tightly before planning the rest of the day. The little boy was obviously anxious and kept close to his caretaker. She asked him where he wanted to go, and he chose the zoo in the Bois de Vincennes.

At first he clung to her, but got gradually distracted by the animals, especially the monkeys. Dizzy wasn't impressed, having visited better zoos in the States. However, her main concern was the child's enjoyment, as she felt she had failed him the previous day.

In fact, she had decided to forgo her own sightseeing plans all week in order to make Marc happy while his cousin was at school. She remembered the article she had seen online about interesting Paris streets and asked the little boy if he would like to go to an outdoor market the next day. She was thinking of the market on *rue Montorgueil* mentioned in the article she had read. But Marc told her he had gone several times with his parents to the *Aligre* market near Mireille's apartment and said it was a special market.

So the next morning, they walked to that huge outdoor market, where Dizzy immediately fell in love with the lively atmosphere. She made a beeline for a colorful produce stand, grabbed a nice red apple on top of an artistically arranged pile, and carefully examined the fruit. The vendor reprimanded her for disturbing his display of merchandise. Marc explained in French to the vendor that his "grandmother" was used to more freedom in the States. Dizzy started singing in a low voice *I did something silly! I won't do it again, promised!* People didn't pay attention to her, being too busy shopping or selling merchandise. The whole market was a perfect place for a free spirit like her.

*****

When Mireille returned from work that day, she announced—through Nicolas as an interpreter—that Marc would be welcome in her office over the next three days. It meant that Dizzy was free to go wherever she wanted. She took advantage of the proposal, the little boy having recovered from his anxiety about her absence on Sunday evening.

Over those three days, Dizzy went by herself to the Eiffel tower and Tour Montparnasse, Montmartre, Louvre museum, and Musée d'Orsay. She didn't miss having Marc as her guide. He was right that English was widely spoken in all those places.

The plan was to leave for Brittany by car on Saturday, with a stop in the historic city of Saint Malo. Nicolas would return to Paris by train on Sunday evening for his school week, while the rest of them would stay in Brittany three more days. Mireille would be on vacation for the whole week.

CHAPTER 14

On Saturday morning, Dizzy heard Marc get up early. He hadn't slept very well because he was excited about the trip to his aunt's house in Brittany. The little boy and his caretaker got dressed and went to the kitchen to eat breakfast. Mireille and Nicolas had already done so. At eight o'clock, the four of them were ready to leave the apartment with light luggage and food for the evening. They went to the underground garage and got into the car, with the two boys sitting in the back.

While Mireille focused on driving, Dizzy watched the scenery and consulted maps of Brittany that she had collected in the past few days at Paris travel agencies. The two cousins chatted in English for a while. Then Marc went to sleep, leaning gently against Nicolas, who spent the time working on some math problems.

When they arrived in Saint Malo, where they had planned to stop for a late lunch and some sightseeing, Mireille parked the car close to the old fortified part of town. First, they went to a quaint restaurant that served mostly fish and seafood. After lunch, they spent some time sightseeing for Dizzy's sake.

The American woman had read about the history of the corsairs and enjoyed seeing the place from which many illustrious explorers had departed for America several centuries earlier. But Marc was impatient to get to his aunt's house, located about an hour away west of Saint Malo.

They finally got to their destination as it was getting dark, but the pink color of the house could still be distinguished.

"*La Maison Rose,*" Marc exclaimed. "The Pink House," he translated for Dizzy.

"Silly you!" Nicolas said. "Mom's house is called Emerald, *Eméraude* in French. Before painting the house pink, she gave it that name because it's on the *Côte d'Eméraude*, the Emerald Coast."

"Why's it called Emerald Coast?" Dizzy asked.

"Because of the color of the sea, at times it turns emerald green around here," Mireille said in French, which got translated into English by her son.

"I don't care, I still want to call it the Pink House," Marc said in a firm tone of voice. "Pink is the color of hope, like you see things through rosy glasses."

Dizzy was glad that the little boy was seemingly aware of the symbolism of colors. She took the chance to remind him that green is the color of nature awakening in springtime and added that orange is the color of fire and wild things. That made her think of Devil. How was he, with Julian as his caretaker? She thought of chatting with her son later in the evening, but remembered that without a special device, her iPhone would not work to call the States.

"Oh well, only one week and we'll be back in Oregon," she mumbled to herself.

In the meantime, Mireille had opened the house and turned on the heat to dispel the humidity left by the rainy Brittany winter. Next, she carried in the food she had prepared in Paris. They were going to eat dinner right away and go to bed very early, so that they could wake up at dawn the next day and get to the Mont Saint Michel before crowds of tourists invaded the place. Over dinner, Nicolas and Marc told Dizzy what to expect at Mont Saint Michel.

On Sunday morning, they agreed to skip breakfast in order to hit the road early. It was a cool day but no rain. While passing through the village, Marc noticed a pleasing aroma coming from the bakery. At his request, they stopped there and bought croissants and portions of *far breton* (a local pastry) to eat in the car.

When they arrived at Mont Saint Michel, there were no lines yet and the parking was easy. They walked to the site and climbed the winding steps to the abbey. Dizzy had heard about the special acoustic quality inside the church and wanted to test it. While Marc and his French relatives were outside getting some fresh air and admiring the view of the channel, she began singing the English words of Mozart's lullaby in her high soprano voice.

A monk appeared and asked her to be quiet, but she didn't understand his French and kept right on singing. Pretty soon some Japanese tourists arrived. One of them approached her and addressed her in Japanese accented English.

"Are you a professional singer? Does the church ask you to perform regularly?"

Dizzy glanced at him. He looked like a man in his sixties. He was impeccably dressed and carried a small camera around his neck. She felt like teasing him.

"Only on Sundays. You're lucky, today is Sunday."

"Really? I lost track of the days of the week. We are touring France in ten days on a bus. The driver is a Frenchman, but he speaks Japanese and English. You know, one day here, one day there." He continued speaking after catching his breath. "I am a businessman from Tokyo. Where are you from?"

"Oregon, in the States."

"I know where Oregon is, on the west coast of America, next to California. I have never been there myself, but I heard that it is pretty. I have a business associate there. Maybe I'll go and visit him." He paused for a while, staring at Dizzy. "What do you do for a living? Singing professionally?"

She was getting uncomfortable. What was the man after? He did not correspond to her image of the stereotypical Japanese tourist: he was too talkative and flirtatious. She decided to tell him the truth, hoping he'd go away.

"I'm a retired nurse, an eighty-year-old widow."

"Eighty years? I thought you were seventy at most. You are in good shape for your age."

"I try to live my life to the fullest. That's why I like to sing, especially in a place like this!"

"May I take a picture of you?"

Without waiting for her answer, he took a snapshot of her and finally went to catch up with his group. Dizzy was relieved to get rid of his attention. At that point Marc and his French relatives came back inside and they toured the church and monastery. But the little boy got tired of sightseeing and wanted to have lunch at the renowned restaurant *La Mère Poulard*. They went down and beat the crowds again. At the restaurant, they ate the famous runny omelet, accompanied by crusty baguette.

They spent some time after lunch in the gift shops. Then they left Mont Saint Michel and headed to Rennes, the capital of Brittany. They had to drop off Nicolas with his schoolbooks, and he would work on math problems before catching a train to Paris later in the day. To Marc's displeasure, his seventeen-year-old cousin couldn't miss a single day of school in his last year of high school.

In spite of the drizzle typical of Brittany, Mireille chose to drive from Mont Saint Michel to Rennes on picturesque country roads. Dizzy enjoyed the sight of small villages with their huge churches and many wayside crosses along their route, indicating that Brittany remained a profoundly Catholic region of France. Mostly she appreciated the signs of springtime: nature reawakening and newborn sheep in the meadows.

Marc was sad to part with his cousin in Rennes. However, he proudly showed off his knowledge of the surroundings on the way to his aunt's house.

"Dizzy, look at the salt meadows."

"What are those?"

He translated Mireille's answer. "They are meadows in which the sea water penetrates. The sheep that are grazing there have a special taste that the French love."

When they noticed bunches of garlic hanging on the covered sidewall of a farmhouse, Dizzy could not hide her amusement and admiration. "Funny, and what an ingenious way to dry garlic! It's also wall art." However, she expressed her disappointment at seeing no flowers in the fields.

"I was hoping to see poppies."

"Too early," Marc said. He translated again what his aunt said in French. "You'll have to come again in the summer. By the way, I heard on the news the other day that poppies are coming back. They mentioned a farmer that uses no pesticides at all. He expects many wildflowers and bees to return to his fields this year."

"I read an article online about it. Could we visit that farm?" Dizzy said. "Where's that?"

"Close…to Paris," Mireille said, trying for the first time to answer the American lady in hesitant English. "You like talk with the farmer?"

"Yes. I'm interested in learning about how he's getting the poppies and bees to return."

"We see him *mercredi*," Mireille decided.

"Wednesday, the day we go back to Paris," Marc said to Dizzy.

*****

There were three more days in Brittany for Mireille, Dizzy, and Marc. The little boy missed his cousin so much that he expressed the desire to leave his aunt's house earlier than planned. When she vigorously protested, saying she wanted to hike along the coast, he turned moody. For the next few days, he refused to join Mireille and Dizzy on their hikes. He stayed in the house by himself, drawing on his pad for hours. The two women felt it was safe to leave him alone, but only had short hikes after lunch.

Dizzy tried in vain to lift the little boy's spirits over dinner by telling him jokes and funny stories. It was obvious that his single goal in France was to spend time with his cousin and feel better about his identity. His caretaker resigned herself, since there was nothing she could do for him just then. But she felt helpless and her joie de vivre was gone. In fact, she started having nightmares, in which Devil had escaped from her house and was lost.

On Wednesday, they left Brittany, and they stopped at the bio farm close to Paris. Discussing the comeback of poppies with the farmer, who spoke fairly good English, Dizzy was reminded of the paintings by Claude Monet. She decided to take Marc the next day to Giverny on the train from Paris. It would keep him busy while Nicolas was in school, and the little boy would probably enjoy seeing

Monet's gardens once more. She made the proposal to him and he accepted readily.

They had a good day in Giverny, admiring the spring flowers in the gardens and having lunch in a restaurant nearby. Dizzy got presents for her granddaughter in a gift shop, all with a poppy theme. Marc asked to return to the apartment in the afternoon because he wanted to spend time with his cousin before dinner.

In the early evening, Dizzy sat on the terrace, wrapped in a shawl that Mireille had lent her. She could hear the two boys having an animated conversation in the living room. She reflected on their visit to France, focusing on the great accomplishments for Marc and herself. When it got dark and a little cold, she got up and started dancing wildly. At the same time, she was loudly singing an improvised song.

> *There once were an elderly lady*
> *and a little boy.*
> *They came from beautiful Oregon,*
> *but they also found France beautiful.*
> *They had a good time in Paris and Brittany.*
> *They were due to return to Oregon*
> *with some great memories.*

It occurred to her only one thing was missing: she hadn't fulfilled her secret wish to do something adventurous in Paris. Would her overnight adventure in Notre-Dame Cathedral count? No, because it wasn't intentional. She had to do something wilder than that to express her joie de vivre.

She went to ask Nicolas if she could borrow the nonmotorized scooter she had seen in his bedroom. He expressed surprise.

"For whom?"

"For me."

"But you're…"

"Old, I know. Don't be afraid to use the word. You know, age is just a number. Excitement and joy have no age limits. I want to ride a scooter tomorrow by the Eiffel Tower."

"You know, you can get one at the Champ de Mars rental place, like Marc and I did the other day."

"But they'll probably have only electric scooters. I want to ride an old-fashioned scooter without a motor. It's safer for me, and more fun!"

"I can lend you the *trottinette* I used as a child. I keep it in my bedroom, just in case." He went to get it and handed it to Dizzy, who started singing.

Trottinette, trottinette, I love your name.
One French word that I'll never forget.
Trottinette, trottinette, I want you.

She stopped when she noticed Nicolas was staring at her and she couldn't help teasing him. "Young people like you want to go faster and faster. Slow speed is good for me. I really want to ride this one, an old-fashioned *trottinette* for an old lady."

"Where will you go to ride it?" Nicolas asked.

"I'll go on the subway to the Eiffel Tower and ride around it."

"But people might stare at you, riding an old *trottinette* without an engine."

"Listen, older women don't care if they look funny."

*****

The next day, Dizzy went to the terrace in the early morning to see what the weather was like. It looked like a typical early-spring day in Paris. The view of the Eiffel Tower made her anticipate the fun ride she would have around it. She decided to wear her flowered dress, a sweater, and red sneakers with white socks. She debated whether to wear a hat and finally decided to do so; it would protect her from either sunshine or rain. Likewise, she hesitated to take her purse but finally took it along, in case she was asked to show her identity papers.

She slipped out of the apartment while everyone was still asleep, and off she went with the *trottinette* in hand. After a short subway ride, she arrived at the Eiffel Tower. She had a ball going on streets around it, riding the old-fashioned vehicle. Some people on modern electric scooters were staring at this elderly lady on a *trottinette*, but she didn't care. She felt so free and exuberant!

When she returned to the apartment, Marc was awake and having breakfast with his aunt in the kitchen. He looked anxiously at Dizzy and saw the vehicle she held in her hands.

"Where were you?"

"Around the Eiffel Tower. I told you and Nicolas yesterday I wanted to go there. It was so much fun riding the *trottinette*!"

"Awesome!" he exclaimed.

He talked rapidly in French to his aunt. Mireille was amazed to hear about Dizzy's new adventure. By then, she knew that the eighty-year-old lady was up to living life to the fullest. As Marc's aunt, she felt good that the little boy could learn from his caretaker to enjoy life as much as possible.

It was the last day in Paris for the Oregonians. Dizzy spent most of the time on the terrace, getting rested for the long trip home and enjoying the view of Paris. Marc went to his cousin's bedroom after the school day was over for Nicolas. Dizzy couldn't distinguish the words of their prolonged talk but could hear the two cousins heartily laughing once in a while.

On Saturday morning, Mireille drove the travelers to the airport, with Marc close to Nicolas in the back of the car. When the cousins tightly hugged each other at the airport, Dizzy felt like shouting "Mission accomplished!" She was really happy again.

CHAPTER 15

At the Portland airport, Marc ran to his mother who was standing in the waiting area. He jumped into her arms and handed her an unwrapped present he was carrying in one hand. "Look at what Aunt Mireille gave me for you! It's a selfie of me and Nicolas. She told me to show it to you right away." Chantal glanced at the framed picture of the two boys on their electric scooters, with the Eiffel Tower in the background. She knew it was a special message from her sister that the cousins had enjoyed their time together.

"You went to ride scooters at the Champ de Mars?" Chantal asked her son.

"Yes, and Dizzy went there by herself yesterday."

"Really?"

"Yes. She asked Nicolas to lend her his old-fashioned *trottinette*. And she had a ball, right, Dizzy?"

The eighty-year-old lady had just caught up with the seven-year-old little boy. She answered while hugging his mother. "Yes, it was a lot of fun. At first I was a bit nervous, but then I got into it. It was so exciting to go faster and faster on the *trottinette!*"

"You really did that?" Chantal asked, seemingly incredulous.

"Yes, and I can prove it to you. A Frenchman with a big camera was taking pictures of the Eiffel Tower for some magazine. He watched me for a few minutes and asked in English how old I was. After I told him my age, he took a picture of me on the *trottinette*. It'll appear in that French magazine, and he promised to send me a copy."

"Did he ask for your name and address?" Marc's mother asked anxiously.

"Yes, but I fooled him. I told him my name was Volcano, and I gave him my brother's address."

"Good for you!" Chantal sounded reassured that her son's care-taker was careful.

She led Dizzy and Marc to the baggage claim. They had already done all the formalities in San Francisco before transferring planes. So they were soon on their way to the Willamette Valley town where they lived, about an hour south of Portland. Once in the car, Marc went to sleep in the back seat and Dizzy dozed off in the passenger seat. When she awoke, after a while, she pulled her phone out of her purse and told Chantal she wanted to call her son. Julian was in his office.

"Hi, Mom."

"Hi Julian, I'm back from France."

"Oh, I thought you were returning tomorrow." ·He paused. "Listen, can I call you back later? I'm working with some clients."

"Tell me, are you still staying in my house?"

"Yeah. Is there a problem?"

"No. I just want to know how Devil is."

"Devil? How would I know? I haven't seen him for several days…"

"What! He's not in the house?"

"I hate to tell you, but he ran away a week ago when Ruby was visiting me."

"A week ago, and you didn't call me…"

"I'd misplaced your number. Anyway, it's just a cat."

"How can you say that? Tell me what happened."

"Mom, I'll call you back later. I told you, I'm with clients. There's a house on the market that's a real bargain, and they seem to be interested."

He hung up, leaving his mother to worry about Devil. When she became restless in the car, Chantal asked her if anything was wrong, but got no answer. Dizzy's phone rang a few minutes later.

"Hello," she said.

"It's me, Julian. Now I can talk for a while, my clients are think-ing it over."

"Tell me what happened with Devil."

"Well, Ruby was visiting me last weekend. On Saturday, I had to work, as you know, so I'd called Liliana, that caretaker you recommended. She came after I'd picked up Ruby. While I was in my office, one of them apparently decided to open the kitchen door. The screen door wasn't locked, and Devil must have pushed it open and escaped."

"That's terrible! My cat is lost."

"Sorry, Mom. But don't worry, we'll find him." He paused for a while. "Can we talk more this evening? My clients want my full attention. I think they want to buy that house."

"OK, Julian. Is Joy, I mean Ruby, in the house with Liliana just now?"

"No, Denise told me she could keep the kid today. Cheaper for me than having to hire Liliana." He sighed with relief. "I'll pick Ruby up on Sunday morning. But I'll bring dinner for you and me tonight. See you later."

"I'm not hungry."

Dizzy realized Julian wasn't listening any longer. She wanted to call her granddaughter right away. She knew the little girl cared much more for cats, especially Devil, than her father did. Maybe her granddaughter would have some information about Devil's whereabouts. But she remembered just in time that Denise had forbidden her to communicate with the six-year-old child.

Dizzy put the phone back in her purse, overcome by fears, and recalled her nightmares about Devil. However, being a positive thinker, she quickly shook off her anxiety and made a plan of action for the next day. She would get up early and walk through the neighborhood in the hope of finding her missing cat. If she had no luck, she would really have to talk with her granddaughter.

After Chantal dropped her off at home, Dizzy was so tired she could hardly drag her suitcase across the driveway. She found her house key in her purse, opened the front door, and called for Devil. There was no answer: he was definitely gone. Dizzy burst into tears but managed to pull her suitcase inside the house. She left it in a corner of the living room and went to bed right away, physically and emotionally exhausted.

When Julian came home later in the evening, his mother pretended to be sound asleep in her bedroom, although she could hear him having dinner alone in the kitchen. She finally went to sleep for a few hours.

*****

On Sunday, Dizzy awoke very early, still being on Paris time. She tiptoed into the living room and noticed the floor needed vacuum cleaning. However, this wasn't the time for housekeeping. She went into the kitchen, unrealistically hoping to see her beloved cat there. Maybe his disappearance had only been a bad dream.

While drinking hot tea, she came to her senses: Devil was definitely missing. She couldn't wait to scout the neighborhood and look for him. The kitchen was dirty and disorderly, but she didn't care. She went back to her bedroom and got dressed. As she reached the front door to leave the house, Julian came out of his bedroom. He wore a comfortable sports outfit, but his face looked tense as usual.

"Good morning, Mom."

"Good morning, Julian. Sorry about last night, I was really exhausted."

"Because of the long trip from France?"

"Maybe."

"Mom, I'm sorry about the dirty house. I had it in my head you were coming back today, and I was planning to clean the house this morning before you returned."

"No problem. I've got more important things on my mind."

"Your cat?"

"Yes. I was just about to go and walk around the neighborhood. I want to ask the neighbors if they've seen him by any chance."

"Listen, I'm going to get Ruby in a few minutes. Denise has to leave early to meet her fiancé. Can I give you a ride?"

"No, thanks. I want to go on foot."

Dizzy left the house. The streets were deserted, as it was still very early on Sunday morning. No neighbors were out yet, so there was nobody to talk to. However, she enjoyed the walk; and on her way, she noticed some springtime plants now in full bloom. But she had bad feelings about her cat's escape. Where could Devil be? Hopefully, he hadn't been hit by a car.

*****

At the end of her walk, the grief-stricken lady chased away negative thoughts when she saw Julian's car in the driveway. Her granddaughter was waiting for her, seated on the front steps. They hugged each other warmly.

"Hi, Grandma."

"Hi, Joy. It's so good to see you again!"

"Have you forgotten her name, Mom?" Julian shouted from the living room. "It's Ruby, not Joy."

"Grandma and I have secrets," the little girl said. "By the way, I think I know where Devil is, but it's a big secret."

"Tell me, Joy!" Dizzy said excitedly. She was really impatient to hear any information her granddaughter had about her missing cat.

"The other day, when you were in France, I made friends with your next-door neighbor…"

"That grumpy old man?"

"No, Grandma. He's not grumpy, he's sad. He told Liliana his wife had died on the day you went to Paris."

"I knew his wife was very sick. Poor man! But tell me, how did you meet him?"

"Last Saturday, I was here to visit my dad. While he was at work, Liliana and I saw Devil run away…"

"What happened?"

"He escaped from the kitchen. Liliana wanted fresh air in the house. She opened the kitchen door, but the screen door wasn't locked, and Devil must have pushed it open. He ran away."

"Silly me! I didn't think to tell anyone to keep the kitchen screen door locked."

"Liliana saw Devil go straight to the house next door. Like he knew the way."

"Strange!"

"I went to talk to your neighbor the next day. He started to tell me how much his wife loved cats. A few months ago, when she got really sick…"

"What?"

"I can't tell you, it's a secret. Harry made me promise not to tell anyone."

"It's about Devil?"

"Yes."

Dizzy felt like shaking the little girl and demanding that she spill out the information she obviously had about Devil. But the grandmother realized that was no way to behave. She thought of running next door to find out where Devil might be, but she recalled seeing no car in the driveway just a few minutes earlier. The next-door neighbor must be away. He might have gone to church on a Sunday morning.

Suddenly, Dizzy had a brainstorm: the presents from France would distract her granddaughter and she might accidentally reveal her secret.

"I brought you a few presents from France, Joy."

"Where are they, Grandma?"

"In my suitcase. I haven't unpacked yet."

"Can I help you?"

"Sure."

They went into the living room and unpacked the suitcase that was still in the corner. Joy started opening all her presents one by one. She especially liked the ones with a red poppy theme from Giverny. But to the grandmother's despair, the trick wasn't working: the little girl hadn't spilled out her big secret.

*****

In the afternoon, Dizzy was feeling restless. She decided to keep looking for Devil in the neighborhood. She asked Joy if she wanted to come along, and the little girl readily accepted the invitation.

It was a nice spring day. They walked slowly on the sidewalk, observing the springtime flowers, as they called Devil every once in a while. Suddenly, Dizzy sensed that somebody was following them. She turned around and saw an elderly man carrying an orange cat in his arms.

"Devil! My babe!" she exclaimed, grabbing her cat and gently rocking him in her arms. She recognized her next-door neighbor, although he looked different from the grumpy old man she had first encountered a while ago. At that time, he was hostile, chiding her and Sam for intruding in his front yard.

She didn't know what to make of this new encounter with her neighbor. She flashed back to a strange dream she had, the first time her cat had escaped. In her dream, she and a nice elderly man ended making friends with each other, after he brought back Devil to her. Could that man in her dream be her next-door neighbor by any chance?

Dizzy came back to the present when the man greeted her with a smile. "Hello, you're back from France! After meeting your son while you were away, I stopped taking care of your mail. Anyway, you hadn't asked me to do so. But last week Julian forgot to take in your empty trashcan, so I did it." He turned to the little girl. "How are you, Ruby?"

"Hello, Harry," she said. "Now, can I tell my grandma the big secret?"

"Go right ahead!"

"Harry told me last Sunday that his wife used to love cats." She yawned, obviously tired by the fast turn of events. "Please, Harry, tell my grandma the whole story."

"OK." He breathed heavily and addressed Dizzy. "When my wife got really sick, she wanted an orange cat like the one we used to have long ago. I wanted to please her, so I immediately went to the shelter and a few pet stores to find one. Unfortunately, nobody had one this color."

Dizzy was getting impatient: what did that have to do with Devil? Why was her cat in the man's arms earlier? To her relief, he calmly continued his long story.

"You remember when you went away for a couple of days? You had one of your friends take care of your cat, but she let him run away. One day my wife and I saw an orange cat in our front yard, looking hungry. I knew it was yours. Harriet told me to let him in and feed him in the kitchen. Poor woman was already really sick. She was getting around in a wheelchair."

He choked up before resuming his story. "She wanted to pet your cat after I fed him. So I brought him to her in the living room, and she fell in love with him. He was the exact color she wanted. When she got the idea to keep your cat for a few days, I couldn't say no to her, she was so sick!" He choked up again. "When you returned, I heard you calling your cat on the street. After a while, I felt bad and tried to convince Harriet that we had to return the cat to you. She finally agreed, and I dropped him on your doorstep."

"So you were the Good Samaritan! I tried to find out who had fed Devil so well after he ran away!" Dizzy exclaimed. She looked at her neighbor and felt compassion for him. "You must miss your wife."

"Harriet wouldn't want me to be sad. Before her cancer, she was a joyful woman full of life."

"I'm sorry…Do you want to keep Devil for a few more days? It might be good for you," Dizzy said generously.

"Could we visit my grandma's cat at your house?" the little girl asked.

"For sure. Come any time you want, you and your grand-mother. My door is open. I was becoming a loner, but Harriet made me promise to be sociable."

Dizzy felt relieved and overjoyed. Now the mystery that had haunted her for a long time was solved. In addition, she was discovering a new side to Harry: he wasn't just a grumpy old man after all.

The three of them resumed walking in silence, Devil in his mama's arms. After a few minutes, Dizzy's iPhone rang. It was her twin brother, wanting to welcome her home. They chatted for a while. She was about to hang up when she remembered to tell him about the magazine.

"Oh, Sunbeam, one more thing. You'll receive a French magazine with a picture of me."

"Are you modeling now?" Sunbeam asked jokingly.

"No, but a photographer took a picture of me riding a *trottinette* by the Eiffel Tower."

"Really?"

"I had so much fun! I forgot my age!"

"I wish I had the same positive attitude," Harry said softly upon overhearing her joyful remarks.

Dizzy glanced at him. He motioned to her to continue her phone conversation, and he discreetly walked away. Then she decided to ask her brother to find Sam, and Sunbeam went to look for him. She felt she had to touch base with her friend. A couple of minutes later, Sam was on the phone.

"Hello, Dizzy. What's up?"

"I'm back from France and wanted to say hello. I've got big news for you. The mystery has been solved."

"What mystery?"

"You forgot? You used to tease me about it. I was dying to know who took care of Devil a while ago when he ran away."

"I remember now."

"Guess who it was!"

"I dunno, and frankly I couldn't care less."

"It was my next-door neighbor."

"That grumpy old man?"

"It turns out he's not really grumpy. You remember, the day we went to his yard, he told us that his wife was very sick. Well, she died two weeks ago." Dizzy was silent for a while. When she resumed talking, it was with joy in her voice. "Harry, my next-door neighbor, is actually a very nice gentleman. And he seems to like me. We were walking together…"

"It sounds like you've found a new friend."

"Yes! Are you jealous?"

"No, I'm content with my life at the commune. I might decide to stay forever. Sunbeam and I get along fine, we have a lot fun together. And he's helping me get clean."

"You mean, your drinking problem?"

"Yeah, it's pretty much gone."

"Bravo!" She became emotional. "Let's keep in touch! We're friends forever."

"For sure!"

"Goodbye for now, my friend Sam."

"See you later, my friend Dizzy."

As she hung up, tears were streaming down her face. Her granddaughter came to hug her. At that point, someone knocked on the door. It was Harry, coming to invite his next-door neighbor to a dance for seniors happening in two weeks. Obviously he was keeping his promise to his wife to enjoy life after her death.

Dizzy accepted her new friend's invitation. She flashed back to her premonitory dream a while back. Everything was falling into place. She now knew the Good Samaritan's identity, and her beloved orange cat was back! Her good friend Sam had found a new home at the commune. Marc had a successful visit in France and was on the way to overcome some of his identity problems, providing relief to his mother. Even Julian and his daughter were on the right track, despite their family drama.

Harry noticed that Dizzy was crying and he hugged her gently. She responded by putting her head on his shoulder and she thanked him again for taking care of Devil in her absence. Then, she timidly suggested to her new friend that they might take some neighborhood walks together. Harry readily accepted and left after saying goodbye to everyone present.

Then Dizzy realized her life was pointing in the right direction, and she was open to reading the signs. After helping other people, she was allowed to think of number one! For the first time since her husband's death, the free spirit was beginning to consider sharing her joie de vivre with a man on a regular basis. She felt ready to turn the page and enjoy new adventures.

ABOUT THE AUTHOR

Jacqueline (Linnette) Lindenfeld, PhD from UCLA, Professor Emerita of Anthropology, is a native of France who has taught and done research in the United States and France (California State University at Northridge, UCLA, Sonoma State University, Collège de France, Université de Paris). Her previous publications—in English or French—in the United States and Western Europe include two novels and six scholarly books. She now lives in Corvallis, Oregon.